Kundo Wakes Up

KUNDO WAKES UP

SAAD Z. HOSSAIN

A TOM DOHERTY ASSOCIATES BOOK
NEW YORK

KUNDO WAKES UP

Edited by Jonathan Strahan

Cover art by Eric Nyquist
Cover design by Christine Foltzer

A Tordotcom Book
Published by Tom Doherty Associates
120 Broadway
New York, NY 10271

www.tor.com

Tor® is a registered trademark of Macmillan Publishing Group, LLC.

ISBN 978-1-250-82393-9 (ebook)
ISBN 978-1-250-82392-2 (trade paperback)

First Edition: 2022

Kundo Wakes Up

Chapter One

Waking Up

Kundo woke as he did most mornings, gasping like a fish stranded on a river bank as the last vestiges of some repeating dream faded, leaving him only with its disturbing physical manifestations: clawed fingers, a light patina of sweat, a rapid heartbeat, and oftentimes, a painful erection.

This cannot be healthy.

Invariably he failed to remember the dream, although he assumed it was recurring. After all, how many variations of an erotic nightmare could his brain throw out? That his brain was malfunctioning was clear. Either his meat brain or his implant: the ubiquitous Echo, part phone, part filter, part processor, the ultimate guide in life, his very own customized Virgil, leading every gobbet around their personal hell with a running commentary and useless bits of information.

Oh yes, it's pretty hot here, 102 degrees Fahrenheit. That aroma is burning flesh with a hint of thyme. . . . This is how it ends for humanity, a slow imbecilic death with full coverage and commentary, everyone a star, no one a fan.

His Echo hadn't received software updates in a while. Was it a year? Six months?

Kundo blinked twice for messages, still his first instinct of the day. Nothing. Nothing personal, nothing from another live human. Nothing even from Karma, the AI running the city, who had been gradually going silent. At first her updates had been round the clock, but over the past few years they had reduced in number, until today, for the first time, there were none at all, no greeting, no report on the weather or hostile-nanotech count in the air. Could an AI stop caring?

He went through the categories of mail—he still thought of them as boxes—and found only spam, archaic advertisements promising space travel to a distant heaven or some extinct multiplayer game. Had he somehow dropped out of citizenship altogether? Was he so utterly irrelevant that even the machines were ignoring him?

Kundo sighed. Already the day was gray. He got to his feet slowly, not sure if he was about to be felled by a massive heart attack, half expecting it. That's the way his father had gone, after all. A cracking sound, like a tree falling; he remembered it vividly because it had startled him awake, the impact of a huge man hitting the deck, blood splattering from his father's broken nose, and he remembered thinking, *Ufff, that's got to hurt, except not really because he's already dead. . . . Could a broken nose hurt a guy whose heart had stopped?* This was a question he had struggled with growing up.

The blinds on his window slid open automatically, filling the room with sunlight. He was very high up, the entire Bay of Bengal stretched out in front of him, pristine-looking, deadly. Of course, this hadn't always been beachfront property, but the water had risen over the past decades, the price for burning fossils for all those centuries, and now he had a great ocean view in a city gently falling to ruin.

He said hello to the bamboo plant by the window, rubbing a leaf gently in greeting, making sure the drip feed was green. He trundled over to the kitchen unit, ordered tea, watched his mug fill with an amber liquid wafting the delicate sandalwood smell of Darjeeling. The kitchen unit was terrible at food. It could barely cook rice and dal, but it made a superb cup of tea, superior even to the priceless real Darjeeling tea leaf that Kundo had once been in the habit of drinking, in his heyday.

He sat in his rocking chair in front of the window, under the dappled shade of the fledgling bamboo, and looked out. The fumes from the mug swamped his face, creating a fragrant mini sauna. There were no ships in the bay—the port had closed long ago—and now only errant seagulls graced the shore, a rare sight. Karma had ceded anything beyond the seawall long ago.

Still, he liked looking out, far into the ocean, and then down to the oceanfront promenade, the great walkway atop the seawall, which in years past would have been crowded with vendors and people. The numbers had dwindled, of course, as more and more people left the city—left or died, Kundo had no idea—but this morning he saw only a few stalwart little dots moving around.

Left or died, that was the question on his mind these days. His wife, for example, had left for sure, because there had been a note, one that clearly stated, "I'm leaving." One year, 236 days ago. Or one year and 237 days if you counted the day she had written the note, which was presumably the night before, since he had woken up to find her gone. If she had made up her mind some time before, if it had not been a spur-of-the-moment leaving, then, of course, the count would have to be revised upward. It was impossible for him to determine the exact moment she might have decided to leave, even though he routinely scoured his memory for signs of disaffection or some seminal instance of revolt.

Like a prisoner, he constantly fretted about the count of days, even though his effort altered nothing.

Of course, he had looked for her, bewildered, wanting

first her return, then an explanation, then just a conversation, or failing that at least some kind of instruction as to how he was supposed to proceed. For example, their collection of books, so valuable, printed on real dead-tree paper, how were they to divide them? Which classics did she want to keep? Surely that Jane Austen gilt-edged one? It was an anniversary present from him and she had treasured it. She had appeared to treasure it. By one year and day 237, he was no longer certain of anything. He wanted her to keep it, but perhaps that was tactless? Evidently she wanted a clean state. Was his presence so terrible that it would pollute even their most beautiful treasures? How could someone abandon a favorite book, or the bamboo plant, for example?

She had disappeared, and he had not been able to find her, despite his resources, so the question always was: left or died? Had the note been a metaphor for suicide? Or perhaps she had actually left with the intention to make a life somewhere, with someone, and subsequently been murdered? Or simply died in the wilderness, at the edges of the city where there weren't enough people to throw up a proper microclime? She wasn't outdoorsy like him, did not have the skills to go foraging.

He couldn't imagine that she would feel the need to deliberately hide from him. He had never been a violent man, something she knew well. In fact, most of the violence had come from her, albeit not physically. Still, what threat had he represented, what possible reaction could she have feared to disappear so thoroughly? These were the grooves his thoughts inevitably ran in, grooves deepening in his mind until they were proper train tracks, inexorable, repeating lines that resisted change.

He skipped breakfast for another cup of tea, settled back into the armchair again, and lost track of time watching the waves breaking. At high tide, the thin strip of beach disappeared completely and the waves hit the wall, sending up a white froth. Street children no longer played on the wall. They had learned the hard way that the froth could kill.

He could empty his mind like this for hours, just sit and breathe. It was meditation, but one without purpose, unless total abnegation of thought counted as a purpose.

The lack of messages disturbed him. Nothing from his wife, nor any of his friends, of course, all of them drifted away, and now not even the city was bothering to acknowledge him. Had he died in his sleep? Was he, in fact, the one who had left? He glanced at his mental calendar. He had last checked it three days ago. Three days gone without record. Had he slept the whole time? No wonder he was woozy, confused. Had he eaten at all? Suddenly he felt a ravenous craving for the beef curry sold near the foot of his building, the illegally parked cart that served food that had certainly never come out of a standard kitchen unit.

It was raining outside, a slight drizzle, and the air quality was fine, but he decided to put on his expedition outfit, for he knew from experience that once outside his feet might take him further afield. The city appeared to be in its death throes, but that was misleading. It was only sloughing off its old skin, the cardboard-box citizens with their boring lives, hamsters bereft of their wheels, rat racers who could not accept that the track was gone. What the city would become next was the real question. This had interested Kundu once, this evolution in front of his eyes of a mammoth organism that did not even know it was alive. It had been his passion even, documenting it.

Perhaps she had left because of it, perhaps he had lost track of time and, by extension, of her, once too often. But she'd had her own life, hadn't she? Her own secrets and hobbies and friends. The game she played incessantly. Had she been fucking them, the gamers in her crew? Secret gamer orgies, her lithe body pawed over by horny adolescent boys? He had never seen them in real life, but he always assumed gamers were pimply faced teenagers, although he knew logically this must not be true; statistics showed that almost 80 percent of the people living in Chittagong gamed casually, and fully 38 percent were considered hard-core.

He had hired a hacker to find the crew, an old acquaintance he could trust. No trace, all three of them were gone, guys aged seventeen, thirty-two, and forty-five, unconnected by anything other than the game they played. Hassem the cyber-eye had at least turned up their names and pictures, their meat identities, although no addresses. Hassem the genius was the last resort, after the police had glanced at his note and scoffed, after all his friends and neighbors had disavowed any further insight into her whereabouts.

So, of course, the faces of those gamers haunted him, and thoughts rose unbidden of them banging his wife, their cocks in her simultaneously, slaves to her will.

Over the past year, however, the raw immediacy of the sting had faded. He could bear to look at a game screen without feeling that roiling nausea, the acid wash of chagrin. In his more zen moments, when his well of self-hate was exhausted, he even wished them bon voyage, hoped they were all together somewhere better, some place full of laughter and companionship and blue skies. When his mind was sharp, he would stop to consider why *all four of them* had disappeared (different days in the same month). Was he so fearsome an adversary? She could have just eloped with them in some polyandrous menagerie, just told him and moved out, and, worst case, he would have whined at her, stacked up her message boxes, perhaps waited outside her new crib with pathetic flowers and a song.

Plenty of people went off in groups for sexual escapades. What the hell else was there to do nowadays, anyway? It was just sex. He could have lived with it. Whatever her plan was, the one unavoidable truth was that he had not been asked to join, not even considered for it. His inadequacy, either physical or psychological, was clear.

Predictable thoughts, running the same tracks a hundred times a day.

Hunger intruded, and for a moment he focused on dressing himself for the great outdoors. Black slick pants, double-layered synthetic, self-healing for punctures. Full-sleeved T-shirt with membrane seals at the neck and wrists. A gray set of gloves with gecko grip, which could be activated with a double tap. Same with the soles of his boots. Useful for climbing over ruins or not getting blown away in a freak hurricane. Coastal weather was unpredictable, despite the best efforts of microclime tech. He took one of her scarves and wrapped it around his face and neck, a tasteful gray one made of the wool of some extinct mountain sheep. It smelled of her perfume, or so he imagined. In fact, that was a lie; it only smelled of illicit cigarettes now. Goggles, helmet, and coat, all of them made for frontier work, away from the city where the air itself was deadly and invisible nanotech could sneak into your body and kill you.

He felt a rush of optimism. It had been weeks since he had gone out properly. The coat had his brushes and paint in long pockets down the right side, and tightly rolled canvas down the other. It had been almost three years since he had painted, but there was always hope.

Chapter Two

Free Beers

He took the elevator down. Thank god it still worked. Many of the apartments in his building were abandoned. He supposed Karma would close it down one day, and make the last few holdouts move to something more compact. Everything still worked though, and soon he was outside, in front of the curry cart.

"Beef bhuna and white rice," he said.

"Kundo Shaheb, how are you? It's been days. I was worried." A middle-aged lady ran the cart. She knew absolutely everyone in the executive quarter.

"I'm fine," Kundo said. "Just lost track of time."

"All alone up there, you should be more careful."

"Yeah." He started wolfing down the curry. He'd often eat at the cart counter, if there wasn't a crowd. "It's extra good today." His wife had hated the curry. Something about the smell of turmeric. What kind of Bengali didn't like turmeric? She used to watch him eat at the cart through binoculars and make acid jokes about how one day he'd run away with the curry lady. *That was love, wasn't it? You wouldn't watch someone eat through binoculars otherwise, would you?*

"Kundo Shaheb, when are you going to paint? Remember you promised?"

He had once offered to paint a mural on her cart, in return for lifetime free curry. He had offered it as a joke, but she seemed to think it was a great deal, and reminded him almost every time now.

"I will, I promise."

"I even have a design ready," she said.

Kundo sighed. He hated commissions.

She brought out a picture of a bizarre eagle-headed man, torso festooned with a zebra pattern of burns, some kind of folklore creature that escaped him. There was a stylized eye on top of his head. *The Eye of Horus? An Egyptian god in Chittagong?* Who knew what mythology these provincials followed nowadays? The great calamities of the past century had churned out all sorts of black magic and peculiar superstitions, the veneer of rationality only surface deep and so easily rubbed off. It made him despair sometimes.

"What the hell is that? He's got weird legs."

"It's Horus," she said, with a deep breath laden with secrecy. "Our savior is coming, Kundo Shaheb."

Great. I'm taking religious advice from a curry lady now.

"He's got funny legs, this savior. It looks like he's cut his own off at the knees and attached someone else's full legs to the stumps. It makes no sense. Are you sure you're going to sell more curries with this kind of picture on your cart?"

"If you open your eyes, you will see more than Karma," she said.

"I have not painted in a long time," Kundo said. "Not since she—"

"Such a shame," she said. "Such a famous artist like you, I can't believe she left you like that."

Tactful as ever. And hardly that famous. I doubt anyone even remembers me anymore. Certainly my agent doesn't. If the curry wasn't this good I don't think I'd ever come down this way. Bloody woman can't stop talking.

Then, to make him feel bad, she gave him a free beer, and had one herself in companionable silence. *Bloody mind reader.* Of course, no one ever stopped at one beer. He bought the next round, and they took turns getting rounds, and by the fifth he was tipsy and they had already started blasting their favorite songs from the 1980s, which seemed to be the world's repository for cheesy music, as if everything cringy but compulsively singable had been compressed into a single decade.

They were halfway through "Wake Me Up Before You Go-Go" by Wham! when a gaggle of lunchtime executives suddenly turned up, talking loudly. The cart lady flipped off her sound box and straightened up into chef mode. Kundo slunk away amidst hard, derisive looks. Everyone else was more or less dressed in fashionable suits and had some kind of executive job, it seemed. This neighborhood had once been expensive and it still retained that cachet. They probably thought he was a drunken hobo, with his scavenging gear. No doubt some security drone would turn up soon to gently usher him away.

Yeah, your suits wouldn't last three minutes in an orange-alert zone, boyos.

The curry had settled his hunger and the drinking had made him crave society. He let his feet take him around the city, the ground level not crowded, at least in this area. Many pedestrians preferred the basement tunnels below the streets, with their conveyor-belt efficiency and protection. In many ways the wealthy had gone underground and left the surface to the freaks and outcasts of the city. Of course, there were the mansions on the hill, that little slice of paradise where the truly wealthy lived, behind their multiple layers of protection, but that was a different world.

Here in a forgotten commercial district, there were tall buildings around him, semiabandoned, semisentient. He felt like an ant walking between giant glass pillars, ignored by everything but liable to be pulped any minute by some absentminded mechanism. His feet took him away from the seawall, toward the more dilapidated parts of town. Men dressed like him began to appear, heads encased in helmets or cowls, heavy goggles around the eyes, every seam and join coated with auto adhesives. What were they doing out here? Scavenging, black-marketeering, god knows what. A lot of the buildings here had been stripped down, useful things pried out, and a certain amount of urban foraging was tolerated. Why not, since so many people had left or died? There were real problems, after all. Storms. Waves of mutant nanotech from the bay. Superbugs that hit meat as well as electronics. Karma had neither the inclination nor the wherewithal to send her drones out for petty crimes.

He reached his first stop, a squat, small-windowed Disera* building, resembling a bunker, revealing much about the architects of that time; no one had time for airy frontage when the sky itself was trying to kill you. The building actually sloped downward, with many of

---

* Disera: Disintegration Era, approximately fifty years or so in the past, when global systems collapsed under the weight of errant nanotech, climate change, severe disruption to trade, and complete abandonment of labor, fossil fuels, and rare metals in the face of molecular fabrication and other techs.

the apartments below ground level, the upper floors left for communal living spaces. He knew the code for the front gate, his Echo reaching out a tendril automatically with the password.

Walking through the circular hive-like corridor, he found it more dilapidated than usual. Only the zeros were left in this building, he could tell. It would not be long before it was abandoned. It had been a respectable address only a few years ago. Now it seemed only the desperate or the criminal lived here. Hassem was wealthy, but he preferred anonymity, like most of his ilk.

He stopped at the unmarked door of the hacker, and pounded for a few minutes to no avail. The screen on the door was disconnected. Nothing stirred behind the door.

Nonplussed, Kundo went to the neighbors, a family with a small baby. He had met them several times. The lady opened on the first bell.

"You!" A curly haired head peeped out.

"Hi, Mrs. Bandar. I was looking for Hassem."

"You're about three months too late," she snorted. "Wait here. He left a note for you." She closed the door and he could hear her rummaging.

Three months? Has it been that long really? Kundo waited awkwardly in the hallway. Eventually she reopened the door, thrust out a handwritten letter. Hassem had a deep distrust for electric communications, almost never used his Echo; that was normal for hackers. He had been somewhat of a calligraphist, practiced in the ancient arts of cursive.

"Do you—"

"I don't know anything. He just upped and left," she said. "Look, I don't wanna know, either, whatever shady shit you two had going on, all right? Just take your letter and fuck off."

"Sorry. Sorry to disturb you. Thanks for holding onto it for so long."

Her face softened a bit. "No. It's okay. He wasn't a bad guy. Just had a really weird lifestyle. He used to help me out a lot. I wish we had some regular neighbors, you know? Some families with kids. Guess you can't be choosy when you're on zero."

Kundo had the grace to look embarrassed. He actually had a shitload of points from those gallery shows long ago. Aficionados in other cities collected his work for hard cash. He was considered a cultural icon in Karma's books. Most people thought he was dead, apparently.

He found a nearby cafe. They were serving three hundred varieties of coffee from a vat dispenser. The bulbs grew directly on the table like some weird tree sprouting drinks. He ordered Javanese mocha espresso and a Kenyan-blend cappuccino, and found that both had the same muddy taste, one slightly milkier than the other.

This was not a particularly good neighborhood.

The letter was brief.

Kundo. Haven't seen you in a while, man. Hope you're still alive. Anyway, I owe you a final report, even though you never came back for it. I pinged you six months ago with a development, but you never responded. Guess you're over it. I think I know what happened to your wife. The funny part is, I can't tell you shit. Really sorry, man. I liked you, you're a good dude. Anyway, don't take it personally. It's got nothing to do with you. Guy like you ought to be famous, touring the big cities, pulling chicks. My advice? Pack your shit and go to Dhaka. Go to Kathmandu, it's paradise over there. Hell, go to London, heard they got one of your paintings in the Tate Modern. Whatever. I'm leaving. Sorry, man. Don't look for me. It's kind of sad to think that maybe you're the only one who might. I'm sure that hadn't crossed your mind, but if you're tempted, just don't. The place I'm going is not for you. Khuda hafez, my friend.

Chapter Three

Bad Buzz

Kundo spent the next twenty minutes dissecting the letter and sipping two more cups of gross coffee, ruining the lunchtime buzz completely. Handwriting analysis with the help of his Echo confirmed that the letter was indeed written by Hassem, using an ink pen on thick old number 32 bond paper, which had once been used for notarized documents. Being a forger of ancient deeds, it was no surprise Hassem would have a variety of such materials. Was it a clue? Hassem often wrote on pen and paper, using dead drops rather than trusting electronics. *I think I know what happened to your wife.* Why would the hacker say that and not tell? Why leave no clue at all, and then pretend to be a friend? *Khuda hafez.* "God be with you," with the Persian inflection, the old way of saying goodbye, now lapsed into formal usage. Why the formality? Why the warning not to keep looking? Was it a suicide cult? *My friend.* They had not been friends. Kundo had known Hassem for a while, but until he had hired him, they had barely spoken five words. Even over the last two years, their interaction had been desultory, a few drunken nights of bonding, perhaps, the rest of it dry discussions over dataflows and tracking algorithms. Hassem had said it himself; it was sad to think Kundo had been the man's last link to humanity. *Is this what they call friendship now? This gossamer link between two people?*

Almost unbidden, he started walking back to the hive apartment. More banging on the door, and this time Mrs. Bandar opened with a scowl, her curly hair forming a messy halo around her head. Her baby was stuck to her hip, pawing at her T-shirt, which was stained with a variety of gloop.

"What?"

"Sorry. I really need to talk to you. Can I come in?"

"No! Why?"

"Please, Mrs. Bandar. It's about my wife and Hassem. People just . . . going missing."

The anguish on his face must have been real, because she opened the door a bit wider. He glanced inside and winced at the mess.

"Look, Kundo, I don't care about your stupid wife or stupid Hassem. People go away all the time. Why would anyone *want* to stay in this hellhole?" There was a break in her voice as she gestured to the cramped living room behind her. "I've got bigger problems. So please. Just stop bothering me."

"But surely you or Mr. Bandar, one of you must have seen something? Some clue as to where Hassem went? Look at his letter. Please just read it. It has a finality to it. Like he's going to die, or leave the earth or something."

Mrs. Bandar sighed. She grabbed Kundo and pulled him inside roughly. It smelled of freshly baked cookies and laundry in the small room, a lovely aroma at odds with the dingy interior. She didn't bother offering him a seat—there was clearly no room on the couch anyway—so they stood facing each other, the baby held like a buffer between them.

"There is no more Mr. Bandar," she said simply. "He left six months ago."

"He disappeared?" Kundo asked. "Like Hassem? It must be linked!"

"Not disappeared, I said he left," she spat out. "The bastard went to Dhaka for some business deal, and never came back. Apparently found a new girl there. Told me to stay put, 'I'm coming back, Fara, don't worry, Fara, a few more months . . .' Piece of shit. Still calls every month with some lame excuse, and I can hear some other chick in the back laughing it up. *Excuse me* for having a kid and getting fat."

"Sorry. Ummm, right. So sorry. Not fat at all, of course. I mean, you look delightful."

"Yeah, right. You wanted to know. I'm stuck here in this shitty building, which is now like almost completely abandoned, and Karma says the next basic allotment suitable for a baby isn't up for six more months, and who knows, it'll be even worse, maybe. I'm a zero. My husband pledged my karma points to borrow hard cash, fucked off, so yeah, excuse me if I don't worry about your precious missing people. They probably fucked off to Dhaka, too. Meanwhile I have to walk twenty blocks a day to get food my kid won't puke up, from a free dispenser, because this GODDAMN KITCHEN UNIT ONLY MAKES TOFU. The great thing is I'm losing the baby weight fast because I'm GODDAMN STARVING."

"Hassem was—"

"I DONT GIVE A FUCK ABOUT HASSEM!"

Kundo took a step back and still got a face full of spit. Miraculously, the toddler just gurgled placidly between them and waved her pudgy fist.

"Sorry," Mrs. Bandar said, her free hand rushing to her mouth. "I haven't spoken to anyone for three months, I think. I'm going crazy talking to the baby. Sorry, it's not your problem. In fact, Hassem used to come around sometimes, babysit so I could, you know, take a bath in peace. He left without a word, though. At least you got a letter."

Kundo felt a rush of sympathy for her. "It's been months since I spoke to anyone either," he said. "I shouldn't have bothered you, Mrs. Bandar. I apologize."

"Call me Fara." She looked around ruefully. "Why are we standing? I'm sorry, I just did laundry, it's not so cluttered here normally. The filters taste funny so the bedroom is full of mineral-water bulbs."

Kundo raised a hand. "Hey. Hey. Fara. It's okay. Can I take the baby for a minute?"

Fara handed her over doubtfully, and then relaxed when Kundo made her giggle.

"I've got her. Why don't you take a moment. Umm, you know, whatever."

"Are you telling me I need a shower?" Fara sniffed herself and laughed. It was a heavy full-throated bellow that made Kundo grin in response.

"Okay. So shoot. What do you wanna know?" She perched on the arm of a couch, and invited Kundo to do the same on the other side.

"Read the note first."

She read it with an arched eyebrow, her expressive face running the gamut of emotions.

"Sounds like suicide, man. But a bit too cheerful for that."

"Right? Am I crazy? It sounds almost like he—they—have all gone off on some secret space voyage or something."

"Maybe they were picked to colonize a new system!" Fara said. "Maybe Karma has a spaceship and she's sending only the best, and we're like the shit left behind!"

Kundo smiled. "You like sci-fi, huh?"

"Love that shit. I'm a big nerd."

"Did he say anything? Hassem? About where he was going?"

"Nope."

"What about the day he gave you the letter?"

"He seemed normal. I don't remember it well, I was distracted, the baby was teething. He came over, said if you ever dropped by and he wasn't in, I should give you the letter. Then two or three days later I realized he was gone."

"How?"

"I have authorization to his place, I actually went and checked." She looked at Kundo's face and laughed again. "It's not like that, you silly man. You think I'm gonna sleep with another dude and risk another demon baby?"

Kundo laughed. "Sorry. I'm a prude, I guess."

"I had his key and he had mine. He used to babysit. I'd drop her off at his place sometimes for an hour or two. Sometimes I used his gaming rig to let off steam. Or he'd pop in and hang out for a bit while she was sleeping so I could go out and shop. Anyway. I thought he might have had a heart attack or something. I mean, he was really putting on weight near the end."

"Can I search his place?" Kundo asked.

She hesitated.

"He's gone. For good, I'd say. I want to know where. Why."

"It's just, um, he left *everything*, you know. He tidied shit up, but there's like a lot of . . ." She looked down. "Like really weird porn. Other illegal-looking tech. Weird gaming couches. And a stash of old-school downers. I snooped."

Kundo frowned. "What are old-school downers?"

"You know, Valium, Xanax, that really old shit. They're super valuable now. I mean, you can order newer downers or fab them black-market, but that ancient shit was stronger. I guess they were way more depressed back then." Fara laughed but there was a manic edge to it. "I know. I take one a day. One day I'm scared I'm gonna take the whole lot. Joking. Joking."

Kundo took a deep breath. He looked around the room. There was nothing hopeful about this place. The air-alert level was permanently on yellow, one ministep from orange. An adult could shrug off yellow, but a baby? All the time?

"Fara, you need to get a nanotech synthesizer. Something to help scrub the air."

She stared at him. "You think I don't know that? What part of zero points do you not get? They don't hand out priceless pieces of equipment to losers like me. . . ."

"Oh, I'll get you one," Kundo said. "I've got points."

"Fuck your charity, big-shot artist," Fara said.

"Help me, and I'll get you an air scrubber *and* water purifier. No more having to carry bulbs of water all day."

"You're a piece of shit, you know that, Kundo?"

"I *need* help. I can't do this alone. I'm desperate. Please, Fara. You knew Hassem. Much better than me. Please. Look, I'll buy you the equipment either way, we find anything useful or not."

"Just like that, huh? Out of the kindness of your heart?"

Kundo shrugged. "I got points and not a single thing to requisition."

"Bullshit. I'm not going to fuck you for it. If that's what you're thinking."

"I'm married. Still. As far as I know."

"Fine." She shrugged. "Let's search his apartment."

Chapter Four

Dragon's Pit

Despite their somewhat lengthy association, Kundo had never actually been inside Hassem's lair. They had met at local bars, gotten drunk, and, Kundo realized, talked mostly about *his* pathetic problems. Hassem himself had divulged no personal truths.

They stepped into the little foyer, which was an ordinary receptacle of shoes, coats, goggles, and the other geegaws of a modern traveler living in a dodgy neighborhood. It was grimy. The steel barrier beyond was also coded shut, and far sturdier than a standard door. Hassem had been paranoid.

Fara breezed through this portal as well, and they stepped into a strange blue-scape, a twilight nimbus that jagged his senses with vertigo. Fara's apartment had been depressingly familiar, a coda to an overwhelmed zero mom. This place, with the same footprint, had a definitely nonstandard interior. As far as Kundo could tell in the dim light, Hassem had knocked down the walls himself, creating a roughly open python space that stretched around and coiled into itself, following lines of equipment, thick cables, ellipsoidal screens, and weird-shaped haptic couches.

There were no standard rooms, no bed, no kitchen, no obvious bathroom; everything interconnected with alien logic, as if Hassem occupied the entire apartment in one go like an overgrown octopus in a tiny tank.

"You used to leave your kid here?" Kundo burst out without thinking.

Fara glared. "She loves it. It's like a magic playground for her."

Indeed the baby was making herself at home already, crawling unsteadily into a kidney-shaped gaming couch particularly configured for her. Within seconds she turned on some flashy touch screen and started cooing.

"He worked here." Fara pointed to one major configuration, and then to another setup behind. These were arranged in apses, semicircular lobes of equipment. "And played here. Um, I wouldn't sit on the play couch if I were you."

Kundo crouched in front of a huge rippling fabric screen. His clumsy jabs and questing Echo failed to bring anything to life. "Is the power off?"

Fara stomped over. "Here." She blew onto a pad and the sail-like cloth sparked up. "It counts the particle signature in your breath. Impossible to replicate. Hassem never skimped on tech."

Kundo watched, fascinated, as intricate images started moving in front of him, a kaleidoscope of surveillance data configuring itself into different visual patterns, unsorted pictures, dates, numbers, and words, a deluge threatening to scour his mind. It was almost art, like an Escher painting made up of actual live data.

"I don't understand how this works," Kundo said.

"Pattern recognition," Fara said. "He had a condition. Partial prosopagnosia. Face blindness. He couldn't recognize faces very well, not even his own face sometimes."

"I didn't know that."

"So he put an implant in his temporal lobe to fix it. His fusiform gyrus, he said. He gave me a lecture on it once. It didn't really work. He was still shit at recognizing people. But one of the side effects was that he could read raw data like a normal person reads facial expressions."

"Wow."

"Yeah, he was smart."

"I can't make head or tail of this."

"No one can, other than him. Or Karma, I guess."

"Karma hasn't answered my questions for the last ten months," Kundo said. "And I'd say most of this data is illegally obtained."

"You stay here long as you like," Fara said. "I've got to feed the kid."

Kundo settled into the couch, felt it tighten around his body, and a weightless sensation took over. A cowl folded around his head, soothing away peripheral vision, and his pupils dilated as he fell into a visual trance. It was strangely relaxing, letting the data wash over him, even though his brain was not configured to make sense of it.

After several hours, he actually fell asleep, and when Fara woke him up he was oddly refreshed. The apartment had no windows. It was so dark he couldn't tell whether it was day or night.

"It's morning. You slept through the night," Fara said. "You looked pretty comfortable so I didn't wake you."

"I don't sleep well at home," Kundo admitted. "This was . . . fine."

"Hassem's vat is out of stock," Fara said. "You want breakfast, you're gonna have to eat whatever I've got."

Which isn't much. I've noticed the slop you eat. Everything good goes to the kid, I bet.

"Let's go to the bar around the corner," Kundo said. He was ravenous. "On me. Air shouldn't be that bad this early."

Fara shrugged. She dragged her fingers through her hair. "Let me get dressed then. Can you mind Sophy for a minute?"

Sitting back on the couch, the baby—toddler?—gurgling in his lap, he felt a peculiar surge of optimism. *It's the child, of course. We're hardwired to feel love and happiness around babies. And we never got to have one of our own. She had refused at first, when we just got married, and then I lost interest when it looked like I was going to make it big, and then it was just too late for us, maybe. Why had she never asked again, why hadn't she insisted? Why hadn't I?*

It would be so easy to slide into Fara Bandar's family, become the missing puzzle piece, drop this ridiculous investigation looking for people who didn't want him, save his powder for someone who cared. He could see it, he'd solve her problems slowly, laugh and joke with her until he became a friend like Hassem, a necessary crutch, and then one day she'd waver and he'd declare his love and they'd live happily ever after. . . . *But is that all we are, shifting pieces, fitted into whatever niche is handy? Do they just expect the rejects like us to make do, to make up new stories to fit our circumstance? Fuck that.*

"Let's go." Fara had changed into a roughly ironed outfit, her hair tidied up. She looked a hell of a lot better put together than Kundo, still in full scavenger gear.

"I'm not sure they're going to let me in." Kundo smiled. "But let's go."

The bartender was hesitant at first, nervously fingering a home-defense switch behind his counter. Then Fara and the baby registered and he flashed them a smile. He was a handsome young man with a vaguely feminine air.

"Kid needs a drink, huh?"

"Breakfast, please," Fara said. "Thought you wouldn't mind the baby, this early. No customers yet."

"Sure, sure, you're always welcome, Mrs. Bandar. Good to see you again. And Sophy, of course. Been a while."

"Yeah, not much reason to party," Fara said. The bartender gave her a warm look, half crush, half sympathy.

They took a secluded booth, and Kundo keyed in generous portions of everything, enough food to last them a couple of days.

"You get anything from the workstation?" Fara asked after a few minutes. She ate quickly, without tasting, like a person who had survived on synthesized tofu gloop for a long time and wanted the meal over with as quickly as possible.

"Not really. I can barely remember anything I saw. Just pictures. He had some of my wife, some new, some so old that even *I* hadn't seen them—so he was being thorough, anyway. He said he had a development six months ago, pinged me . . ."

"Why didn't you respond?" Fara asked.

"I don't know. I was out of it. I don't remember the days. It feels like a dream, days merging together, lost all that time.

Had a breakdown, I guess. Shut off completely."

"Sorry," Fara said. "I know what that feels like. I wish I could switch off, drift away. You're lucky, at least it's just you. If I didn't have Sophy I think I would have just jacked into a game and not come out."

"It's pathetic, I know. I'm not the first guy to ever get dumped. Anyway, I picked up the threads again recently. To be honest, Hassem was the only one left working on the disappearance. I believe he knows what happened to her. I think they're both alive. I think he's gone to the same place as her, something about the investigation triggered his own decision."

"Kind of like they found some magic wonderland, huh?" Fara said. "All the cool kids are there and they won't give you the key. Poor Kundo."

"They didn't give you the key either," Kundo said, stung.

"My husband's wonderland is in between some tweenie's legs," Fara said. "I know exactly where his key is. Good fucking riddance. He was a lousy fuck anyway." She held her palms over her baby's ears. "I know, I know, I swear all the time, I'm gonna stop by the time she's old enough to understand."

"Studies show that people who swear are more trustworthy," Kundo said.

"Fuck off. They left us like we were trash, Kundo.

Garbage. When we first got married he was stuck to my ass. Couldn't get enough. After I had the kid it's like he couldn't bear to touch me anymore. We're the people no one wants. Why don't you get that?"

Kundo's face must have mirrored her hurt because she clamped her mouth shut.

She got up, started putting the extra food in boxes, automatically packing every scrap. She stopped after a moment, embarrassment flooding her face.

"I'm sorry. I didn't even ask if you wanted to pack your food." She slid the boxes across the table, toward him.

"It's okay, it's for both of us. I was planning on going back to Hassem's."

"It's fine, Kundo," Fara said tiredly. "You don't have to drag me around feeding me. Like I said, I enjoy losing the weight."

"I can't make any of his systems work," Kundo said. "And I don't understand Hassem's tech at all. You'll have to help me, you know, breathe on everything. I know you're busy. You're doing *me* a favor."

"Sure, whatever."

Chapter Five

Voyeur Blues

Later, throughout the day, with Hassem's innards exposed like a gutted animal, Kundo felt like an ancient oracle, divining the truth from spilt viscera. Even with Hassem's peculiar prosopagnosiac way of reading data, Kundo was able to glean the ebbs and flows of his life, the dry corporate work he did sometimes, the dirty surveillance looking for cheating lovers or scammers, clients hunting for vengeance, clients seeking to escape. Hassem had his passion projects; Kundo's wife was one of them; perhaps it was the absolute, traceless manner of her disappearance that had intrigued him. After all, he himself had been a master at erasing data, at evading the system. Or maybe it was just the voyeuristic pleasure of hunting an attractive woman.

Kundo felt himself sinking into the images, most of them unknown to him, grabbed off random feeds, of her doing everyday things while he was not around, moments he had no idea of. There was a series of her at an expensive seed shop, looking at a small potted plant, a real live one to keep at home. He remembered her fascination with trees, with green life. She touched almost all of the leafy samples in the shop, her eyes closed, as if her selection was entirely by touch. Kundo remembered that first sapling she had brought back home; they had spent hours finding the perfect spot with the right amount of light, and she had whipped out a measuring cup to water it, lips furrowed in utter concentration, as if one extra drop would have doomed the tree.

The images of her out in the city were all from the early years. Near the end she had stopped leaving the apartment. The gaming had become more pronounced, her purchases shifting toward more and more arcana; their karma points had been entwined, and plenty accrued in that account from his art, more than she could spend. He had not cared, never checked her excesses. His own mind was obsessive, his life in and out of fugues, and it had not seemed strange to him that she had also started to mirror his psychological landscape. These images were too bittersweet to contemplate for long. He wished he could slip back in time and restart at some of those points, lose his self-absorption. He blundered on.

In one of the side terminals he found something more disturbing: reams of backed-up feeds of the apartment next door, hyper-close stills of the Bandars, and then mostly of Fara, a clinical mapping of every inch of her, every second of her day. Privacy was a costly thing these days; most people just accepted that any single moment might be exposed, but this was obsessive even so, betraying a yearning that was palpable.

Fara's snooping had been desultory. There was no way she had seen this. Kundo was tempted to erase it all, and he made a half-hearted try until he realized that Hassem's systems were resistant to change, far beyond *his* abilities, at any rate. It occurred to Kundo that Hassem could have deleted it himself, this entire archive devoted to his neighbor, had he wanted it gone. Devoted. There was something deeply emotional about this.

He had left it as a shrine, his goodbye note. Did everyone spend their lives yearning for people who couldn't see them? Had his own wife felt that, the weight of his regard for everything else but her? He had loved her. He loved her still. *She* had withdrawn from *him*. He had never once considered that she might have had an internal life as rich as his own, that in the moments he had been in the ecstasy of art she had not just been hovering in a holding pattern awaiting his return. She had been engulfed in her own concerns, and they had consumed her eventually.

It seemed to him that all human stories were depressingly the same: catch and release, a giant puzzle with every piece jammed together in the wrong way.

He returned to Fara's for lunch, feeling the full weight of Hassem's accumulated psychic grime. Who wanted to take on another human being's full load of sin?

She had tidied up her place, set the table, some instinct for normalcy returning. They ate the leftovers in awkward silence, using her best plates and cutlery.

"Okay, Kundo, what the hell is the matter?" she asked. "You find something scary?"

"Creepy."

"What was it?"

"Fara, he had a lot of feeds of you. Like a shrine. He had cameras in your apartment."

"What?"

"There are livestreams from every room, multiple angles."

Fara groaned. "Oh god. He helped me put up a camera in the nursery, so I could watch the baby if I had to go out in an emergency. I have the feed linked to my Echo."

"I think he put in a few extra. Um, in the bathroom and stuff. Your closet. Over your bed."

"Fuck fuck fuck fucker!"

"It's none of my business. I'm not judging. But your breath is keyed into his security. You can walk through his doors. I think maybe you were closer than you're saying. . . ."

"One time. *One time.* It was right after the dickhead left. I was drunk, he was babysitting, I went over, we watched some weird ancient porn and then we fucked on his anti-grav weightless couch thing. Okay? You want more gory details?"

"No."

"It's none of your fucking business."

"You're right. Sorry. I think he was in love with you, in his way. I don't know what you'd call it. I'm not one to talk, what the hell do I know?"

"I knew he had a crush on me and I used it," Fara said after a long moment. "I used him. I was desperate and when I needed help he always came through. I'm not proud of that. I guess the voyeur shit was the price. He was so sad and alone. He was my only friend and he never said bye."

"He left it there for you to find one day. Kind of like a love letter."

"Oh god. That's not love, that's just creepy and weird and scary. It's gross. You saw all of it, huh?"

"Enough. I didn't know how to delete or skip his feed or I would have."

"Okay, can we pretend you haven't seen me in every embarrassing situation possible and just move on?"

"When I was much younger, I used to paint live models. Men, women, often naked, doing regular everyday things. It got to a point when my immediate reactions were no longer erotic. . . . If I can explain myself better, I observed lines, ellipses, planes of skin and muscle. It wasn't like seeing someone naked. It wasn't real. I don't know if that makes you feel better."

"Um, yeah, whatever, I'd still like to keep my ellipses to myself, if you don't mind."

Kundo smiled. "Understood."

"And we're not going to talk about this again, right?"

"Sure."

"'Cause I'm going to take a sledgehammer to that screen of his."

"I don't think that's going to get rid of the data, but sure. . . ."

"So you find anything useful? For your wife, I mean."

"Nothing. But I was thinking. You mentioned he used to game. My wife was a huge gamer. *World of Final Fantasy 9000*. She had a crew, three guys, they all went missing as well. . . ."

"Oh." Fara's expression suggested *problem solved*.

"Yeah, I thought that, too, of course. It doesn't add up, though. I mean, why disappear? She could have just walked out with them. People get divorced all the time, it's not like I could have stopped her. Why not say anything, if it was something as mundane as an affair?"

"Um, maybe 'cause she didn't give a shit? Ever thought

of that? Maybe she just couldn't be bothered to deal with your blubbering and the five-hour conversations and the guilt," Fara said. "Trust me, that happens more often than you think."

"Blubbering," Kundo said. "Yes, maybe I would have blubbered and pleaded. That does sound tiresome."

"Kundo, you're a real wimp," Fara said with a smile. "Can you just grow a spine?"

Irrationally Kundo remembered a series he had painted of men with metal spines. It leached the venom from her words. "I think I was a different man before, you know, the breakdown. I had a spine then. I'm not sure that was better."

"Anyway, Hassem wasn't that kind of gamer. He only played retro stuff. Mario Kart. Cartoony, twentieth-century stuff, real simple. My kid loved playing them. Hassem was a collector."

"He didn't play *FF9000*?"

"Nope. He hated that shit. Used to go on about how the golden age of gaming was gone, and the stuff now was just derivative fuckery with better bandwidth."

Kundo felt himself deflating. Best theory, shot down.

"I'm lost then."

"Oh, but what about his mail?"

"I can't get into his messages. Maybe with you breathing on it . . ."

"No," Fara said. "He didn't use e-coms that much. I meant his actual mail. Paper mail."

"Like, he got letters in envelopes? That kind?"

"Yup," Fara said. "Come on."

Back in the blue darkness, Fara navigated a way to the corner, to a cloth-lined box filled with handwritten notes, drawings, opened envelopes, printed fliers. There were compartments, but Hassem's organizing principle, as always, was opaque. They split the pile in two and dove in.

If his feed had been dark, the paper trail was even worse. These were messages people were afraid to put down electronically, from the very basement of the dark Web, requests for awful things, snippets of ongoing correspondence that hinted Hassem had facilitated awful things. Black clinics. Forced body grafts. Children, abused, turned into things. Illegal cutting, gene splicing at grotesque levels. It was a small part of his oeuvre. But it was there.

Fara looked up, eyes screwed with outrage. "I swear I never knew this side of him."

"You said he never left the house," Kundo said. "He wasn't doing these things, Fara."

"But he was helping people to do them. He was teaching them how to hide."

Kundo rubbed his face. "I don't know. How much can we know *anyone*? I can't believe my wife was involved with people like this, in things like this."

"She might not have been," Fara said. "Look at this."

Kundo read a letter written on thick paper, sealed with wax.

"It's a game invitation, I think," he said. "*Black Road.* That's all it says."

"You thought a game tied them all together," Fara said. "Maybe this is it."

"The paper." Kundo pulled out another sheet, the letter Hassem had left him. He examined them. "It's the same paper. Thirty-two bond. Same exact ancient paper. He left us a thread. Maybe subconsciously, but he left us a small thread. We have to find this game."

"It says nothing, though: no URL, no link, address, or even shop name." Fara blinked a search on her Echo. "No mention at all of *Black Road* as a game. It sounds like a hoax."

Kundo felt a flush of excitement. "Hassem used to sell old paper. For documents. Forgeries. He told me once. It was his best earner, he said. I bet he sourced this paper for them. These *Black Road* people. He must have known them."

Fara held up one small hand. "Hold on there. You're basing an awful lot on two pieces of paper."

"I'm going to go outside," Kundo said. "Foraging. People don't use paper much anymore. Someone will remember. Someone on the street will have heard of the *Black Road.*"

Chapter Six

We Game with the Devil

Kundo took to the streets, this time with a purpose. An ill wind blew before him, clearing the alleys, sending the street people scurrying for shelter. Over the years, Karma had driven most of her valuable flock underground. What came from the sea was not always defensible. Only the leftover people stayed above, like ticks on a giant's scalp. He hunched his shoulders, hoping the seals on his suit held. He couldn't remember the last time he had topped up the adhesives in the joints, or oiled the supple faux-leather bits. Were they critical? His Echo had stopped receiving messages from the manufacturer, which had gone bankrupt sometime in the last two years. It seemed everything recognizable was shutting down. Was the atrophy around him accelerating, his degeneration a mere reflection of the universal state, and he was simply too narcissistic to notice?

No. My pain is precious. I cannot let it go. This is all the emotion I have left. I will find out what happened. Other peo-

ple fade. Their pain and their joy fades. Mine will not. Because I hoard it. Because I paint it inside my skin and hang it on the walls of my bones. I won't just blow away with the wind. If the pain goes then I will disappear entirely.

He walked far into the red zone, hardly caring, into the worst gaming hells, the places that put in cheap grafts for fun, places with a Taiwanese autosurgery kit fitted in the back room, ready to change your topography. Fun and games. There were rumors of slave factories where kids were chained to grind out PvP characters for wealthy gamers. Maybe Karma knew; maybe Karma didn't care. He wandered for hours, finding old people he had touched during his initial frantic search. He had been incoherent then, he realized. Many of these people remembered him as a crazy man, wild with passion. They saw him now as a husk, spent, and pitied him. Many people had moved on; the gamer world was always in flux, living on the edge of forbidden tech, and he had never been a part of it, never fully initiated into their masonic communications.

There was a place deep inside the orange zone near the Karnaphuli River, built on the bones of an old market, the Firingi Bazar, literally *foreigner market*. The Firingi Bazar had been gutted by arson five decades ago and Karma had cleared the space, repurposing old shipping containers into shops. She had given them gratis to local vendors, one of her many community revitalization projects that lingered despite the slow decay of the city itself.

Five years ago Kundo had gone there to paint a gamer, a part of his acclaimed series on human augmentation. The subject was a young man grafting giant inputs into his neck, trying to squeeze the last extra nanosecond of speed out of his spinal cord in a futile attempt to fight the rise of cutting-edge military-spec Echos, of hive minds in Tokyo and rumored human-AI mind melds in space, all of which revved the brain far into the post-human.

There were artists and gamblers in the bazaar, shikh-kebab places, dodgy brothels, opium rooms that were just wall-to-wall mattresses, where customers went in one way and rolled out of the other end three days later. It had been lively and cheerful; men and women recognized him, feted him with free drinks and kebabs, and he sketched a good number of them, passed the portraits around in revelry, making every person look more vital and divine, giving them a little something extra, as far as his talent could stretch. It was a grand day, like a small street carnival.

He never finished that original painting; the boy drifted away eventually, looking comical, like a cartoon figure with a giant socket in his neck. There was something too inexorably pathetic about him to put down on canvas, as if the finality of brushstrokes would have locked his fate in amber.

The shop owner was Hafez, named after the Persian poet, called the Tiger by his fellows for his swaggering gait. He was a dandy with a sharp beard and an iron-topped cane, black marketeer, pirate, ladies' man, procurer of rare items; whispers in the alleys complained he was something worse, murderer and revolutionary, elbow-deep in the blood spilt in the Night Market riots.

The shop was a front and Hafez owned the whole row, perhaps the entire market. He was an uncrowned king, collecting tribute in daylight, dressed to the nines, doffing his hat with urbane menace, dispensing judgment, running an economy Karma had more or less abandoned. His court of desperadoes followed him in full riotous color, and if he gazed ruefully at them from time to time, he seemed to enjoy their campy exuberance just the same.

The Tiger pulled Kundo into his orbit, wined and dined him, the square turning frenzied at night with excess energy, offering a plethora of raw, illicit entertainment. In the end, sated, Kundo drew Hafez instead, using the half-light of dawn to capture a wistfulness peculiar to very violent men.

Arriving at Firingi Bazar now, he sought those old faces, half-remembered, and found no one he recognized. This place was sleepier, sluggish, many of the container stalls shuttered, the riotous smell of food dialed low, replaced by the blandness of low-grade vat tofu. Most worryingly, the courtesans had left, and taken the revelry with them.

The old shop was there in the corner, however, grimy and derelict. He pounded on the door, and a kid came out, barely fifteen and belligerent.

"Yeah?"

"There was a man here before, with a moustache," Kundo said. "The Tiger, they called him. Five years ago, maybe?"

"Yeah."

"He still alive?"

"Yeah."

"Does he still work here? Can I see him?"

"Nope."

"What happened to him?"

"He got sick. He's at Chitts Medical."

"I'm sorry to hear that, he was a great man. You run the shop now, huh?"

"He's my uncle," the boy said. He spat on the ground. "Shop barely runs."

"You game, though, right?"

"Who doesn't?"

"Ever heard of *Black Road*?"

"Who hasn't?"

"Me. I haven't. Tell me about it, please. I couldn't buy it anywhere."

"'Cause it's hidden in another game, ain't it?"

"What other game? Who runs it?"

"It's the devil's game, man. You win the *Black Road*, you get invited to move on. Like the lottery, ain't it?"

"What's the prize? What's the end goal?"

"To get the fuck outta this world, ain't it? Devil has a way out." The boy shook his head. "Look around you, man. Who the fuck wants to stay in this drowning city?"

"How do I play it?"

"Fuck you, old man. Leave me alone." The boy pointed toward the sky and hissed, "*We're being watched, fool.*"

"I have points," Kundo said. *Watched? By whom?*

"Fuck your points," the boy said. "We live and die zeros here, motherfucker."

"I want an invite. Get me one, and I'll give you the latest haptic suit, no strings attached."

"No fucking way you're getting an invite, loser. Haptic suits? Really? That's like for kids."

Kundo stared at him helplessly. "At least tell me who gives these invites. What do you mean, it's the devil's game?"

"The DEVIL," the boy said. "His game, his invite."

"Like Satan?"

"Sure. Shaitan. Lucifer. Horus. The devil, man, the burnt guy with horns and legs that don't fit. He has to call you."

"Horus!"

"What?"

"That thing you're describing. The burnt thing with the legs. Horus. I've seen pictures of him. On walls in abandoned places. What is he? How is he connected to the *Black Road*?"

"Black Roaders and the Eye Cult. Two different groups, man. The Roaders play the game, and the Horus cult follow the Eye. It's tech versus black magic, man. Everyone looking for the exit. Some in the middle think Horus runs the *Black Road*."

"I can't find anything about either of them on the Echosphere."

"It's all in the dark, man, you gotta be able to *see*. Square-ass motherfuckers like you just live on the surface. Get the fuck back to your green zone, asshole."

"What happens to the people who win the game? Where do they go?"

"Piss off." He again made the sign for drones overhead, thieves' cant.

"Okay. Okay." Kundo turned to leave. "Your uncle, Hafez Shaheb, what room is he in? In the hospital?"

"General ward. Why?"

57

"I did a portrait of him once. I remember that day clearly. One of the last good days, maybe." Kundo patted his side pocket absently, feeling the tight roll of canvas. "I'd like to see him again. He was my friend."

"Wait. You drew that picture?"

"Sure."

"Was it all black-and-white shit? At dawn?"

"Charcoal sketch."

"He loves that picture, man. His mind is fucked but he lights up whenever he looks at it. Takes it wherever he goes. You're Kundo."

"Yes."

"You painted that shit for real?"

"Yes."

"I'm gonna show you something cool. Come with me."

Chapter Seven

Centipede Love

They hit a series of winding alleys, delving deeper into the orange-alert zone, until even Kundo's sluggish Echo started mouthing off an alarm, promising dire consequences unless he returned to his recommended area. Kundo sequestered it with a flick of his mind. Most places were yellow to orange these days. Still, in these narrow streets, where tilted remnants of ancient brick buildings largely blocked the sky, there were greater signs of life: basement windows giving off light, graffiti on the walls, children playing games on abandoned surfaces.

Now he saw it. There were pictures everywhere. Eye of Horus. Legs. The cart lady had asked him to *look*. In this hidden route the boy took him, he paid attention and images slid into his peripheral vision, half-complete drawings of eagles, sly juxtapositions of iron bars that looked like misshapen legs. The zebra pattern of burns mirrored on walls tattooed with drone fire.

The boy forced him into a parkour course until Kundo's knees creaked and he had to beg for a rest. The Fringe people feared surveillance. There had been riots before, most notably the Night Market ten years ago, which Karma had quashed with more or less violence, depending on who told the story. There was talk of three thousand people disappearing overnight from a vigil, mostly young kids, either gone home or dead, who knew? For a while, crude posters of the alleged dead had appeared in public spaces, duly torn down by police, then replaced, but eventually the furor had died down, once one or two of the missing wandered back.

The Fringe remembered every single bullet, nourished every sliver of revolutionary fervor; all they craved was a human enemy, a dictator worth hating, not this insipid machine who fed and clothed them with one hand and mowed them down with the other, police drones jacked in the air, all the while flooding their Echospheres with gentle admonishments to wear sufficient skin cream and drink plenty of water.

Just when Kundo felt his lungs bursting, they finally returned to a regular neighborhood, one inhabited by people of fixed abodes, at least, boasting commerce and the trappings of normal life. There were ground-floor shops here, touting repairs and maintenance. The shells of machines hulked in piles outside each frontage—old industrial robots, commercial vats from restaurants, smart gantries and cranes from the building-boom days—all of it stripped down, the metal and ceramics taken out to be melted. It cost money to dispose of large equipment; there were regulations and taxes involved, karma points docked for impropriety. This was a smart work-around, a win-win situation for both local businesses and the tinker clans who lived here, if one ignored the hazardous alchemy.

Chittagong had long ago gotten rich on shipbreaking, and now, when the ships had stopped coming, the old breaking instinct was turned on itself, tapping against the city like a woodpecker's beak, threatening to rip out its own innards if it wasn't fed.

They stopped before one large shop, boasting the name KARIM AND SONS in faded letters, followed by an improbable list of accolades. It apparently specialized in air scrubbers, for a large number of these were stacked up outside, some still beeping in panic at the perpetual orange alert.

Karim Senior was inside behind a long oiled workbench, vacant-eyed, watching something on Echo. He was a large bald man, with faded tattoos in Bangla lettering across the visible stretch of shoulders and arms. He glanced at the boy and frowned. He pointed up silently. This man, too, was paranoid.

"Chachaji."* The boy touched the man's hairy arm. They were blood relatives, it was clear.

"Serhan," Karim Senior said. "Why have you come here in daylight? Are you mad? Who is this man?"

"He is Kundo," the boy said grandly. "The painter."

Karim Senior accessed something on Echo and grunted.

"He wants to see gamers in action. We weren't followed. I went through that street where the Echos don't work. He made the painting. Of Hafez chacha. The black-and-white one in the hat and the cane."

Karim Senior's face softened. "Okay. Five minutes. Don't bother anyone."

A metal rack clicked and swung back into a black tunnel, releasing a whiff of frigid air.

Kundo followed the boy in. It was dark but comfortable enough with Echo cranking his eyes up to maximum dilation. The tunnel was short and cold, pleasantly so after the dire heat outside. It opened into a large room, filled with haptic couches, noisy with the whirring of cooling jets. About twenty gamers lay prone, eyes twitching, slathered in gel. The oldest was a middle-aged woman, the youngest a seven-or eight-year-old boy. This

---

* chacha: uncle

place was clinical and high tech, completely at odds with the shabbiness outside.

"Tournament death match in *FF9000*," Serhan said. There was a trace of pride in his voice. "A special one. Just two weapons, one for each hand. No magic, no potions. Weapons and armor have to be standard issue. Pure skill. These are some of the best players in the city."

"They're playing *Black Road* then," Kundo said.

"*FF9000* doesn't know it, but *Black Road* is piggybacking off them. That's why you can't find it anywhere. It's hidden in plain sight. You need a special link to get into the death match."

"Why are they here, though?" Kundo asked. "Underground, I mean."

"This shit ain't legal. We have a PMD dampener here."

The "PMD" was shorthand for "personal medical device," the little bone-shaped insert they all carried in their spines, the thing that regulated all their systems, kept the mutations in check, released molecule-sized nanobots to repair damaged tissue. It was what made them godlike; the PMD also kept the body ticking over on the nanotech count, producing those semi-biological airborne particles that were necessary to equilibrate the microclimes. Each healthy human contributed particles to the air, donations to the microclime run by the city. PMD was both boon and tax rolled in one, illegal to tamper with in any demesne ruled by Karma.

"I don't know what that means."

"It creates a field that slows down PMDs within a certain radius. Without alerting the cops."

"Wouldn't that make people sicker?"

"This is a clean room. This is why we charge the big bucks."

"So why are they dampening PMDs?"

"So the virus can take over."

"I don't follow."

"The gaming virus, man. If you wanna go deep into the game, you need this shit. Once the worms take hold of you, you can stay under for days, if your PMD lets you. You wanna try, or what?"

Kundo walked along the "infectious" couches, his skin crawling, as the boy described the process of going under with great enthusiasm. Each figure was prone, wrapped in flat hairy arms extruded by the couch itself, as if giant centipedes were trying to consume its occupant. The arms were pale boneless tentacles, organic enough to jack his heartbeat way up. Microscopic hairs on the arms telescoped into the skin, creating an almost complete auxiliary nervous system; this was cutting-edge gaming, a far cry from holograms or cowls or the old lucid-dreaming rigs. The hairs released viral molecules into the bloodstream, preventing immune-system responses, allowing an almost full symbiosis between couch and player. The bodies trembled sometimes.

His Echo flipped up gamertags over each body. Lord-Nelson. Ogawarajones. Shahedk. SapientApe. Storied names with stratospheric kill counts and hordes of followers. His wife would have known more about them; she had followed the boards avidly. *FF9000* was the big game, the world game, and its protagonists were celebrities. He had imagined gaming to be a social event, people gathered around a screen, perhaps, laughing and shouting. This place was a mausoleum, the inhabitants caught in a half life, furiously still.

He imagined her sitting in one of these illegal couches, wrapped in her bone-white centipede lover, shuddering in obscene centipede orgasms, a lover that never lost interest, never talked back, the two of them ambered in some sylvan fairy tale, hand in hand forever.

Was real life that truly bad for you, then? I wish you had said something. Or perhaps you did and I simply ignored it.

He remembered the gear she had accumulated over the years, top-of-the-line gaming-ware. There had been augments to the Echo, drugs to enhance neuron speed, high-end electronics. They had been well-off, able to afford the nonsense, and she had spent freely. All of that accumulated junk seemed tawdry compared to the worm sarcophagi.

"Only two shops like this in Chitts. Maybe fifty centipedes total. Fuck them implants and shit, that's all over. It's all viral gaming now. You wanna win, you gotta feed the worm, man. You wanna try? Ogawarajones set a world record, man, he's been under for sixty-five days now."

"How's he still alive?" Kundo asked.

"Virus slows down your body. The centipedes feed you nutrients, leach out wastes. The couch recycles shit. It's like being in space."

"And he's *paying* you?"

"Sure. Got his karma account hooked up direct. He told us not to wake him."

"What if he runs out of points?"

Serhan scoffed. "He ain't gonna run out. Got enough for two hundred thirty years. The fucker's generating points even as we speak, people watching his old gaming feeds and shit. We ain't puttin' scrubs on the couch, man. I told you. This shit is cutting edge even in Seoul."

"Old feeds? So he's not casting what he's playing now?"

"Nope. *Black Road* shit is encrypted. No casting, no livestreaming, no comment. Sixty-five days in the worm, man, that's a fucken record and I can't even tell anyone!"

Kundo shuddered. "You couldn't put me in your centipede coma even if you paid me."

"So you ain't a gamer, then," the boy said, disappointed. Perhaps he dreamt of making a sale. "Why you want to play *Black Road*?"

Kundo flipped him a picture over Echo, his wife eating breakfast in a cafe, the sun filtering through her hair like a halo.

"Pretty lady."

"I'm trying to find her. Did she ever come here? Use one of the couches?"

"Nope."

"You sure?"

"This is the family business, man. I'm here all the time. The implant place is just a front. Take appointments. Sometimes some old-school fool comes along for some implant and I plug 'em. Serious gamers quit that shit two, three years ago." The boy pointed at the couch. "You know how that works? You get butt naked and I slather you in gel. Then you get in and the 'pedes wrap around you and little hairs stick into you everywhere and you go to sleep. It's freaky the first time. I talk 'em through it. Trust me, I'd have remembered if your wife came by here."

"Okay. What about this guy?" Kundo sent him another picture.

"Hassem?"

"You know him!"

"Hell yeah. Everyone knows him. He's a freak and a

half. You know he can read data with his eyes? He bought a couch, man, six months ago. Only sale I've ever had. He used to drop serious points on hardware."

"You delivered it?"

"Sure. To his place. Looks like a cave, all dark and shit. He was teched up, man, he had some serious warez. But the centipede blow that shit away."

"Thank you. Thank you," Kundo said. He grabbed the boy's shoulder in an awkward hug. "I owe you one. Thank you!"

"Serhan!" the boy shouted after him. "My name is Serhan!"

Chapter Eight

Domestic Bliss

When he reached Hassem's apartment it was the dead of night and he realized that he had been gone for over thirty hours, roving, without sleep or food other than the random scraps in his pocket. Exhaustion hit him so hard that he couldn't imagine the trek back to his own place. Hassem's was locked, the security holding firm against everyone but Fara. He checked her door, touched the pad with his fingers, and found to his surprise that he was keyed in. She had, perhaps, anticipated this very situation, saved herself being rousted in the middle of the night.

He let himself in gratefully, found a blanket and a pillow on the couch. He stripped off his roving gear in the corner, into his T-shirt and boxers, briefly considered taking a shower before just collapsing into the couch and passing out immediately.

Much later, he woke up to the sound of the kitchen unit whirring and Sophy smacking his face with chubby fingers. When his eyes flipped open she gurgled with glee and bopped him on the nose.

"I figured you'd crash here," Fara said over the noise.

Kundo rubbed the sleep from his eyes. He felt ravenous, alert, better than he had in months. No dreams. Even his sinuses were clear, remarkable after so many hours of roving. He glanced across, noticed the ever-present orange air alert was gone; the meter blinked at a steady green. Fara stood in front of him, her stance oddly stiff.

"The machines came. I installed them while you were gone. I thought you'd forgotten about that shit." She looked at him. "First time it's ever been green in here. Thanks, Kundo. I mean it. It's the most anyone's ever done for me in a long time. More than that cunt husband of mine ever did. You're probably saving my baby's life. I know I couldn't ever afford it. So yeah. I owe you. Whatever." Her last words were forced out, almost bitter. She was too proud to accept help, clearly too proud to be in the deficit for very long.

Kundo looked down, embarrassed. "Please, forget it. I wouldn't be anywhere without your help. Maybe you don't see it, but you're saving *my* life. I was drifting away, you know, I was disappearing. Whole weeks are missing. I . . . well, I feel a bit more real around you and Sophy. So thank you."

"You stink," Fara said with a smile. "Shower is that way.

Through the bedroom. Don't snoop through my stuff."

"Right. Thanks." He sat up, wrapping the blanket around himself.

He set the jets at maximum power. The alternate gusts of air and water sluiced away the grime, left him with a new layer of skin. Loath to put on his soiled clothes, he ended up snooping, hoping to find the errant husband's outfits. There were none. The bright-red bathrobe on a hook was the only viable option. He put it on and came outside sheepishly.

"No clothes, huh?" Fara laughed at him. Sophy toddled over and started tugging at the hem of the robe, incensed at this blatant daylight robbery. She was fiendishly strong. The robe, already short, began to slip alarmingly.

"Perhaps Mr. Bandar left something behind?" Kundo said, frantically trying to fend off the toddler. Sophy bit him on the calf, with sharp cannibal teeth. What kind of beastly thing was she?

"I took scissors to all his stuff," Fara said, unrepentant. "Sorry. Hmm, okay, there is one thing left."

It was a formal suit, tight-waisted, black silk, the coat reaching back to his knees, slightly loose on him, the sleeves half an inch short. He felt ridiculous, like an undertaker.

"That cost too much money to cut up," Fara said. "I

was going to sell it. You look very dashing."

"I look stupid," Kundo said.

"You never had to wear formal coats before, in your exhibitions and stuff?" she asked.

"Artists . . . they expect us to be drunk all the time and wearing feathers or something. I was fine with T-shirts. Last time I put on a coat was when I got married."

"Of course. Sorry. Touchy subject."

She did not seem sorry at all, Kundo reflected.

"Still, man, you must have been to some grand places. I've never left this stupid drowned city."

Grand places. A memory hit him hard, took his breath away, a trip they had taken together right after getting married, to bejeweled Kathmandu, where a different Karma ruled, one who cared; were they all the same, these machines called Karma, the same mind partitioned to madness?

He remembered his wife walking in a garden, trailing fingers through green leaves and vines, barefoot, her red toenails winking fireflies in the grass, her face wide open with unadulterated joy, and he had thought this was the first time she had let slip a final mask, revealed emotions he had never even known existed. He had felt the urge to paint her, but he knew instinctively that she would not like it, that she'd recoil and he'd probably never see that look in her eyes again. Now, twenty years later, he could still feel the grass beneath his feet, the smell of leaves and dirt, the babble of water falling somewhere, and ineffable sadness came over him with the realization that even if that garden still existed, he would never go there again.

If I could live in a moment forever, that would be a good one, wouldn't it? And if you had enough moments like that, strung like pearls on a string, well, wouldn't that be a life worth having? Worth remembering? She didn't have enough moments like that, not enough for a necklace. Or a collar. It's good memories that chain us to life, after all. If I had given her more of those she would not have left.

"So you found something," Fara said. "I can tell by the stupid look on your face."

You can't read people for shit, Fara. That was a look of despair. Nothing else.

"Ever heard of a gaming couch called the centipede?"

"No."

"It's cutting edge, very dark Web, all the serious guys are using it."

"Okaaaay."

"So Hassem bought one. It's in his apartment somewhere."

"He only played retro games, though."

"Right? Except for one. I think he bought the couch to play—"

"*Black Road!*"

"Exactly."

"And if the couch is still there, then maybe the game is, too!" Fara said.

"Do you want to find out what the fuss is about?"

"Hell yeah, Kundo, let's fucking roll."

Chapter Nine

Certainty of Needles

"Fuck you, Kundo, I'm not getting into that."

They stood before the couch, a nondescript fat slug of tech, vaguely organic. Fara watched the operating video that came with it, and her face immediately fell. The couch, like everything else in Hassem's apartment, readily accepted Fara's biometrics as a key. Kundo looked and, sure enough, there was a PMD dampener nearby, a mini version of the machine in the gamer cave. He checked the air quality and found this section of the apartment to be almost antiseptic green. There was no doubt Hassem had gone deep.

"I'm not a gamer, Fara," Kundo said. "I wouldn't know the first thing to do in there. The boy who sold it said they're running some fight tournament piggybacking off *Final Fantasy 9000*. You have to win to find out what happens next."

"This couch sticks needles into you," Fara said, her eyes wide. "You want needles stuck in your dick, you get in it."

"It's not needles," Kundo said. "It's more like cilia. Hair. And you can't feel anything. I've seen the pro gamers in the den. They seemed perfectly comfortable."

She snorted.

"I won't leave your side, I promise. Just go in for an hour, check it out. I'll keep Sophy with me right here. I can see what you're playing on this little screen. I promise I'll pull you out if you hit anything strange. There's a symbiote mode—you can talk to me throughout the thing."

"Kundo, you know you're the biggest piece-of-shit coward I've ever met?"

Kundo grinned. "I know, I know."

"I feel like a hired gun," she grumbled. "What kind of guy doesn't game at all?"

"I'm a weirdo, I guess."

"Yeah, well, maybe your precious wife wouldn't have fucked off if you'd gamed with her once in a while."

Ouch. Conversations with Fara always extracted a price, Kundo was beginning to realize. Perhaps Mr. Bandar had left out of self-preservation.

"Sorry. I talk too much shit." She held up her hand in apology.

"It's fine." Kundo shrugged. "You're not wrong."

"Okay, it says I have to strip and put this blue gunk all over me," Fara said. "Turn around, don't look."

Kundo moved away with Sophy on his hip. She protested briefly, and then urged him toward her preferred station, which sensed her proximity and welcomed her with the hologram of a miniature panda. She chortled and started playing some complicated air-waving game with the digital toy. He wondered if she was lonely at all, without any children nearby. He supposed there would be schools and such later on.

He glanced back to find that Fara was already in the couch. She was covered in indigo gel, even her face and scalp; she seemed alien, strangely powerful.

"If this hurts I'm going to kill you, Kundo," she said. She covered herself with her arms even though the gel obscured everything.

He tried to smile reassuringly at her as the fat centipedes began to extrude from the couch, but he couldn't repress an instinctive shudder. She glared at him throughout the process. The worms began to cover her in seemingly random patterns, and then cocooned her almost completely. She shuddered once and then her eyes rolled back. Kundo stopped himself from yanking her out. He expected her to start convulsing but instead she settled gently into the couch after that, the tension completely draining from her limbs.

"Okay, I'm in," she said after a few minutes. "It feels weird. Ticklish. The interface is very fast. There's only one game. *FF9000*. There's a death match bookmarked. Encrypted link."

"Serhan said that's the link for *Black Road*, and the devil is watching," Kundo said.

"Devil, huh?"

"Yeah, so don't embarrass us."

He could see her log in with her avatar, stripped down to a basic skin and standard weapons. Her character was a witch queen, similar to her in build and look, something the game engine did automatically.

It occurred to him that Hassem had left the couch open for her use; he must have hoped she would find her way to him.

The arena was a simple black surface, a road that came from a point in the horizon in the starless sky; all around was only empty space, an inky blackness without any means of judging depth or distance. The road itself was featureless stone, about twenty meters wide, the edges falling off abruptly.

There was something ominous about the road and the darkness of the space all around, a wrongness that came through even on the small screen. Kundo had seen the lush rendering of *FF9000*, the painstaking, fantastic whorl on every leaf and flower. It was anathema to the game to have this gaping maw of abnegation, a deliberate absence of surface detail and substance that gnawed at the mind.

❦

It jarred him, made him blink into the distance and try to discern the end of the black road. After his eyes adjusted he thought he could see, far away, a mirage of a city, a promise of horror and abandonment. He wanted Fara to forget about the tournament and run toward it, to see the color of its walls and towers, to bring it somehow into better focus. He knew instinctively that this was a real place, that this darkness was rendered just as faithfully as the most spectacular realms of the game.

"Here we are, it's starting."

Fara walked on with a talwar and a round shield. The one-handed Moghul sword was curved and shimmered with the watery mark of old Damascus steel. Without use of her spells or more exotic powers, she relied mostly on speed. The talwar had a very short hilt, and the angle of the grip encouraged a fighting style of short downward cuts.

The enemy was a player called Malam, a noob armed with dual katanas and dragon-motif samurai armor, one of the default favorites of young men with a Japanese sword fetish. They clashed in the middle in a series of whirling dervish moves. Fara fought with short cuts in a compact style. Block, block, block, cut. Her movements were fluid, lifelike. Malam moved in a herky-jerky fashion; his rig was clearly inferior. Kundo surmised that in these early stages, the centipede would give them an enormous advantage.

Malam attacked with a wild swinging style, flashy circles and jumps. Fara just defended in the beginning, letting him tire himself out. All special and magical moves were disabled in the tournament, a rule that affected Malam badly. In several instances he appeared to be trying a combo that resulted in nothing, muscle memory betraying him.

After a while, when she was sure of his repertoire, Fara started counterattacking. For every blocked hit, she bit back with short powerful blows, downward jerks of her arm that smashed through his lapped armor, often hitting his torso or his thighs, an automatic strike like a thresher. The feed Kundo watched was remarkably lifelike. Each blow drew gouts of blood. He could see three bars on Fara's feed, for armor, hit points, and stamina, reflecting her physical condition. This was the default state, although a lot more bars were available, some of them linked to the gamer's actual physical condition, such as heart rate, breathing, adrenaline levels.

Kundo couldn't see Malam's bars, but he could guess that the samurai was the type of player who depleted his stamina bar with every move. There was an easy pattern to his attacks, an enforced break after each big swing, as if he was struggling to catch his breath.

It was clear that Fara knew how to use her shield and

was relatively safe from all of the katana-scything frenzy. Her style was methodical, practical, and ugly. Far too often Malam would spend all his coin on a beautiful strike that would be blocked, winning minimal damage.

In the end Malam went down from exhaustion more than anything else. The game mechanics reduced his movement efficacy as his stamina zeroed out, and this translated into weaker blows and slower dodges. At this point Malam was visibly panting, his tattered armor heavy on his body, and with a defense reliant on speed, he was doomed. The game even rendered the sweat flying off his face as he labored on.

One blow to his right thigh smashed all the way to the bone, and he fell to his knees. Fara started to methodically chop him into bits with deep downward cuts, until his shoulders were both hanging on by gristle, the scales of his chest plate reduced to bloody strips dangling like some macabre curtain. His weapons fell from nerveless fingers; he was already dead on his knees when Fara cut his head off for good measure, with a relish that made Kundo wince.

After the obligatory fountain of blood the game winked out. There were no words of victory, no music, simply the black road fading away, a faint patina of the city lingering in the horizon.

"That was amazing," Fara said. "This couch is amazing."

"Okay, come out now," Kundo said.

"What d'ya mean?"

"It's a test run, your hour is up."

"But it's fuuunnnnnn. . . ."

"Fara, that's the virus talking. You know the couch infects you, right?"

"I'm an aaaaddict."

"Can you please get out?"

"Okay, okay, grinch, jeez." More inaudible grumbling, accompanied by a disturbing slurping sound as the centipedes withdrew.

Kundo went to pick up Sophy, who started protesting vociferously.

"I've got to get this gunk off," Fara said, muffled underneath three sets of multicolored towels. "It's gross. Let's go home."

"Did you see the city in the background?" he asked, when she had finished showering.

"I was busy, hello," Fara said. Her eyes were shining. "Damn, that was the most realistic fight I've ever been in. Like I could feel the sword shaking in my hands, every time it split his armor. I think I could taste his blood in the air."

"Isn't the arena strange? A black road and a city in the back," Kundo said. "That must be where the name comes from."

"I don't mind trying again. I didn't see the city."

"It was far and very faint. I stared at the horizon and it almost misted into focus, like a mirage."

"You want me to go back or not? I think the more matches you win the closer you get to the city."

"We have to be careful," Kundo said. "The worms might be addictive. Those guys were under for months, the boy said."

"You think your wife's in some cafe, in a couch?" Fara asked.

Kundo rubbed his face. Was it that banal, in the end? A gaming junkie wasting away in a cave? But even normal haptic couches cost money, and the centipede rate was exorbitant. She had stopped spending from their account; Hassem had confirmed she had even stopped claiming basic. What was she doing for money, then? Was she bartering somehow? Was someone else paying for her?

"I don't know."

"I'll tell you something," Fara said. "Once you're in there, it's like a trance. You don't want to come out. You said those big gamers dive deep for months. I can understand that. If I went under that long I don't think I'd ever come back."

"We have to find out more about this game," Kundo said. "And the city."

Chapter Ten

One More Life

"You only get one life."

"Hmm?"

"In the tournament," Fara said. They were eating breakfast in the pub, one of the new routines they had fallen into. "Only one life."

"Right." The food was good. Chappatis and spiced potatoes, something that brought back childhood memories. Anything was better than Fara's vat unit. He had wanted to upgrade it but they already had a great deal of awkwardness about expenses. He was sleeping on her couch and had persuaded her to accept edible food in lieu of rent. He would have stayed at Hassem's but its unearthly creepiness was too oppressive. In any case, the apartment clammed up without Fara, all the systems shutting down without her pheromone signature, since the whole thing was a peculiar nerdy shrine to her.

"So I can't waste it," Fara said. "I'm not like an expert fighter, you get that, right? It looked easy because Malam was a noob and I had the couch."

"You did really well," Kundo said.

"I fought another guy at night," Fara said. "SapientApe. He was better. I won but I took a lot of damage. I don't know how much further I can go."

"So after the first few rounds you start meeting the serious players," Kundo said.

"With better rigs. And eventually someone else with a couch," Fara said. "There's no way we can win this, Kundo, without help."

"I need to get out there," Kundo said. "Scavenging. I need to find the buzz on this devil tournament. Find some Satan-worshipping gamers or whatever. If you win the *Black Road*, you get to play something else, I'm sure of it."

"You get to the city maybe," Fara said.

Kundo paid. "I know you're itching to jump into the couch. Don't."

"I need to practice," Fara said. She frowned. "Luckily I've got a lot more free time since I'm not hauling water for Sophy all day. Don't worry, I can't go under for long anyway. The game ate my babysitter, remember?"

Kundo spent half an hour putting on his scavenger suit, meticulously cleaning it first with help (not really) from Sophy. Her fascination with the goggles made him laugh, and he almost subconsciously started to sketch her, before his mind sharpened into focus and the urge went away. He gave her the half-finished drawing.

"That's an original Kundo, you know," he told her. "It'll be worth something when I'm dead."

She promptly balled it up and tried to eat it.

When Kundo finally hit the streets and edged into the orange zone, he realized he hadn't the faintest idea of where to go, just the urge to keep moving, like a wounded animal. When he was alone, amorphous images of his wife engulfed him, like a cloud of semi-sentient regrets, a cancerous hollowness of anxiety right below his sternum. *How is it possible to remember someone every second, to recall little innocent moments with so much chagrin? Why am I now jealous of her every interaction with other people? I never thought about her at all when she was in front of me.*

Moving helped, so he walked. Above-surface buildings in the orange tended to shift hands quickly, depending on the vagaries of air, nanotech, and Karma's errant eye. Tired police drones staggered around, randomly threatening people but seldom doing much else. He wandered toward the nearest subway station, which was spotless and well monitored. Karma still cared about public spaces. As the water rose every year, he wondered how long that would last.

On a whim he decided to visit his old friend Hafez at the hospital. That man had been steeped in gamer lore.

Was it a stretch to call him a friend, Kundo wondered idly, as the train swallowed him from the platform and whisked him into darkness. It was such a loose word now. Friend. Someone on your Echo list? Someone who shared your feed? Someone you physically knew? As he followed the threads of all his connections, he found them severed at the ends, floating in the air. *This is how spiders die. Their threads break and they fall.*

The subway was still free, and the train duly stopped at all the stations, even though most of the time there were no passengers and some of the stops had to be closed during tidal flooding. People just didn't move around as much as they used to, but Karma apparently considered running the trains on time to be the high-water mark of her reign.

There was a group of three young girls in the cabin, whispering together. His Echo pinged off theirs in polite greeting, an automatic brush between strangers. They ceased talking and stared at him with big eyes, and Kundo remembered that his gear was frightening to normal people. Scavenger. Zero. Scab.

It brought to mind hordes of zeros encroaching on respectable suburbs, scurrying over buildings like army ants, stripping everything, yanking the PMDs out of fallen bodies. *Stay out of the orange zones, kids, or the scavengers will sell you for parts. . . .* He wanted to pull off his mask and smile but it was too much effort so he waved lamely and tried to look nonthreatening.

The train stopped directly at Chittagong Medical, an ancient government hospital lovingly restored by Karma. It was spotless and smelled faintly of antiseptic. With the advent of PMDs, the nature of medical care had changed. Most ailments were treated remotely, and the PMD itself formed the first, second, and third lines of defense. People who went to hospital fell into roughly two categories: those with serious nanotech issues that compromised their PMDs, and elderly folk who needed chronic care but had no family to give a shit.

The latter group was greater, by far. As Kundo wandered in, he found that this was more old-folks home than any hospital he remembered from his youth. The PMD might keep you ticking longer, but it couldn't make you new friends or magic up grandkids. Most of these denizens ended up in the wards because their own families had deposited them here, forlorn centenarians who might spend months without speaking to another human being until they literally died of loneliness.

Kundo shuddered at the thought that he himself was one small step away from this state. He thought about Fara stuffed up with Sophy in their small apartment, barely making it, and realized that they were all maybe one bad day away from turning up here.

The Tiger Hafez was not difficult to find. There was one human receptionist in the entire hospital entrance hall, and he was reading a book in a quiet corner trying to avoid work. As Kundo was in no way related to the patient, he was bounced around automated systems until he landed in front of this individual. The receptionist's eyes lit up at the mention of Hafez, and he even shook Kundo's hand and very courteously guided him to the right ward, Hafez apparently a sort of celebrity here.

Hafez was asleep at the time, his body sprawled across the bed, bedecked in a crimson silk dressing gown, feet encased in fluffy slippers, his hair white now but still combed back neatly, the beard gray and sharply pointed with wax. The beaky nose looked bigger, as his face had grown gaunt. *He's not a tiger anymore,* Kundo thought. *He's more like a raven, or a vulture.*

Several meters away, another cot held a more decrepit patient, muttering silently behind drawn curtains. There were six beds in the ward, all of them occupied. Each bed had a small table and an armchair next to it for visitors who never came. Kundo was the only outsider here.

He sat down. The upholstery was stiff, the cushion still factory-firm. The ward was actually pleasant, with natural light and a view of trees, a faint lavender smell pervading the air and some kind of circular robot vacuuming the floor discreetly; the only things distasteful were the human wrecks in each bed. Of what little Kundo could see through drawn curtains, Hafez appeared to be the best of the lot, and he wasn't half the man he had been five years ago. Much of the vitality, the violence had left him. Whatever he had was eating him away from the inside.

Hafez woke up after a few minutes, sensing Kundo's presence. His eyes were confused at first, darting left and right with nervous energy, but then something clicked and he seemed to relax. He looked almost plaintively at Kundo, in silent inquiry.

Kundo gave Hafez a salaam, a lump of sadness in his throat.

"You are the artist," Hafez said after a few seconds. "I remember." He glanced toward the wall where Kundo's portrait was hung, an elegant dash of black-and-white breaking up the beige monotony.

"Kundo," Kundo said.

"Yes, you are Kundo. And who am I again?"

"Tiger Hafez," Kundo said, startled.

Hafez smiled. "Tiger Hafez. Sorry, that's my little joke. Don't worry, banchod,* I haven't lost everything yet." His hands were like claws, the veins etched green against the

---

* Banchod: sister fucker

skin. They trembled on the white sheets, until Hafez balled them into fists. He pressed a button and the machine in his bed released drugs into his intravenous feed. His words became clearer almost instantaneously.

"I went by the shop," Kundo said. "Firingi Bazar has changed."

"It's finished." Hafez shrugged. "I'm finished, too." He held a finger up to his lips and pointed up, indicating surveillance drones.

"Your nephew told me you were ill."

"The haramis† threw me in here," Hafez said. "Locked me up for life."

"Really?"

"I have advanced Echo Rejection Syndrome," Hafez said. "Along with some rare form of something called Alzheimer's, which basically means I'm slowly losing my memories. Left unchecked I will forget numbers, faces, words, even how to chew eventually. I need the Echo to arrest this. How ironic, then, that my brain is rejecting it."

"I'm sorry."

"Nothing is sorrier, however, than the fact that my matherchod‡ brothers have decided to store me perma-

---

† Haramis: bastards
‡ Matherchod: motherfucker

nently in this ward," Hafez said. "Filled with the insane, the friendless, and the mindless: in other words, the elderly. I daily contemplate suicide, I tell you, but without the right weapons I feel they will simply revive me. Nothing worse than a failed attempt."

"Is it that bad here?" Kundo asked, aghast.

Hafez glared. "The drugs make me cloudy. Look at these stupid bastards around me, burnt out brains but their PMDs keep them alive like zombies. You know a PMD will go on ticking forever, unless you stop it? Human fucking fabricators, that's what we are in the end. Of course, Karma won't kill off the zombies. She can't get nanotech producers this cheap anywhere else. National banchod treasures, she calls us. . . ."

"God, this is terrible. I've never thought about getting old before."

"No one thinks they'll get old," Hafez said. "PMD makes you invincible. No one gets sick, no one gets hurt. Let me tell you, every so-called hospital has wards filled with men like me, just staring at the ceiling."

"And you can't leave?"

"Ward of the state," Hafez said. "Booked for life. They say I'd die out there. Matherchod, people are supposed to die. I've put enough people into the ground to know that. Karma is a motherfucker, Kundo. You think she works for you, but she doesn't. Don't ever forget that."

"They say there are people up in space who've beaten death," Kundo said.

"Yeah, that's not for you or me," Hafez said. "That's fuckers with equity. They live forever. You think they wear the same PMDs we do? You think their bones are making good nanotech for the rest of us?"

"Equity class," Kundo said. "We're just the numbers that make up the world. The aggregate they need to keep things ticking for them."

"Damn right," Hafez said. He sat up a bit straighter. He stared at his portrait for a moment, as if gathering clues from the man he had been.

"Look at me grousing. Seen you after what, five years? I'd offer you a drink, but they took all my good stuff. My memory's going, they say, but I remember that night clearly. You're a single-malt man, like me, but you prefer the Japanese over the Scots, like the heretic you are." He beamed after remembering all of that.

Kundo nodded, a little twist of sorrow in his gut. They had drunk chilled vodka that night, with a dash of black pepper.

"I haven't lost everything yet," Hafez said. "I can't tell time anymore, though, can you believe that? I can't read the clockface. It's the strangest thing. Well, Kundo. Before I doze off again, tell me. How can I help you?"

Kundo felt embarrassed to even ask for help from this

husk of a man, but Hafez was looking at him so expectantly that he blurted it out.

"My wife left."

Hafez looked under his blanket. "She's not here."

"She just disappeared. I'm worried she's in some kind of trouble." *Maybe I'm hoping she's been kidnapped or murdered, because it's much too painful to think that she just wandered away without a word.*

"Kundo, my friend, people leave all the time," Hafez said, echoing his thoughts. "You realize with age that all human bonds are myths. No one is destined to be together. It only exists in our minds. Whispers and cobwebs."

"What's real, then?" Kundo asked. "Love, pain, it's all made up? I refuse to accept that."

"When I was whole, I was showered with love and affection. Hatred, too," Hafez said. "Where has it all gone now, eh? Poof! In the ether. Tiger Hafez, dead to the world. Men who'd cower when I looked at them won't bother crossing the street to spit on me now. When you depreciate an asset down to zero, you have something called scrap value left. That's what we are, Kundo, you and I. Scrap value only."

"Scraps," Kundo said. "Sure. But we have a little bit of juice left in us, don't we? For one more run?"

Hafez straightened his chin. "That we do, my friend."

"There is a game they play, a fight tournament," Kundo said. "It's in *FF9000,* but an arena I've never seen or heard of before. A long black road in the middle of nothingness, and a very faint city in the back."

"Ah."

"I think they played the game, my wife and Hassem both."

"What has Hassem to do with it?"

"You know Hassem? I hired him to find her. He left a note before he disappeared, too."

"Yes, Hassem the hacker. Everyone knew him in the trade. He's fallen into the game, then?"

"You know the game?"

"Yes, of course. The *Black Road,*" Hafez said, "leads to Gangaridai."

"That name . . . what is it?"

"The legendary first city of Bengal, ruled by men and djinn."

"Can you take me there?" Kundo asked, grabbing the Tiger's trembling hands.

"Yes," Hafez said. "Yes. But first, you will get me out of *here.*"

Chapter Eleven

Body Bankruptcy

It was easy getting Hafez out of the ward. Kundo got a form from the receptionist to take Hafez for an "outing." He merely had to acknowledge receipt of the man as his temporary caregiver, a status that Hafez conferred to him with a blink, and then sign a lengthy legal document stating that all ills befalling the Tiger for the duration of their trip would be placed squarely upon Kundo's head, including civil penalties, possible docking of KPs, and even loss of citizenship. Kundo freely signed, although he was certain that the Tiger would never again voluntarily return to this ward.

He remembered a time when he had hoarded karma points, gloating at his karmic balance, a time when the paint had flown onto empty canvasses and then directly into the living rooms of the rich via posh galleries and auction houses, when Karma would check in on him every day and her favors would accrue with metronomic regularity. Lately he had begun suspecting that it was simply a game invented by whoever was in charge—AI or human—to keep them all busy. Apparently even when humans had everything, they needed some kind of hustle to satisfy their inner cravings of self-worth, some method of keeping score.

It took an hour or so for all the eye blinking to be completed, and then Hafez's suitcase wheeled itself in like a cubist dog. The Tiger swung to his feet and started laying out his clothes. Kundo drew the curtain around the bed and left him. An inordinate amount of time later, he heard a hesitant call.

"I'm stuck," Hafez said, from the armchair.

He was mostly dressed, in a spectacularly cut indigo suit, with a rich purple waistcoat and cravat. A smooth bowler hat lay on the bed. He had come undone with the socks and shoes.

"I can't bend that far," he mumbled, his head down.

"It's okay, I got it."

The shoes were beautiful black patent leather, shined to a mirror finish. Kundo laced them up around the silk socks, and then lined up the trouser creases. Kundo heaved Hafez up and gave him his telescoping cane for good measure. The Tiger stood erect, straightened out various folds of fabric, inserted a handkerchief into his top pocket, and gave a sigh of approval.

"Never die in your pajamas, Kundo," he said. "Death is

serious business. Always wear a good suit."

"I appreciate your point, but given my luck I think death will find me in my underwear doing something embarrassing."

"You artists," Hafez said, as they walked out of the ward. "So scruffy."

Hafez, in fact, looked so sharp that even the drones manning the entrance saluted him. They strolled out with élan, the exit only slightly marred by the suitcase beeping along after them in faint panic.

The first order of business was stopping at the nearest human bar—Hafez insisted on being served by a living bartender—where, at exorbitant prices, they quaffed two measures of Irish single malt (a lie since most of Ireland was abandoned) and puffed on some hand-rolled cigars. Hafez's hand shook from whatever neurological malfunction was currently ailing him, and most of his priceless Irish whiskey ended up on the floor. Kundo pretended not to notice.

The bartender started with the inane conversational patter that customers paid so highly for, but a dark glare from Hafez shut him up midsentence. He retreated to the side and discreetly dabbed his eyes with his apron.

"So, you want to visit your family? Go around the old neighborhood?" Kundo asked.

"Fuck no." Hafez gave him the same black eye. "They

left me in a ward, Kundo. I'm just trash to them."

Kundo looked at him, in his sharp suit and his growling eyes, the flush of rage along his fair neck, juxtaposed with his shaking hands, the faint tremor in his frame that betrayed the effort he was making to prop himself against the bar for so long, the minute sips of whiskey all he could manage, the cigar ash trailing along the counter, all accoutrements of a lost age. *At what point are we used up? You're luckier than most, Hafez: you got to be the Tiger for the last sixty years. My sell-by date came a lot quicker.*

"Okay, okay." He forced a laugh. "We'll tear up the town, how about that?"

Hafez smiled. "My friend, you and I both know that the only thing I'll be tearing up are my lungs. It's funny, Kundo, do you know what I crave the most?"

"Wine? Women? Drugs?"

"You would think that," Hafez said. "God knows I've had more than my share of all of that. What I crave the most, Kundo, is to be useful. To do something useful. Irrelevance is our enemy. I've lain in the ward and run through every simulated entertainment invented, and there's a point when you can't tell the difference between what's real and what's virtual. All these years, I was out on the streets, thinking I had the world by the balls . . . I could have been a game junkie on a dirty mattress and lived the same exact life."

"You'd know the difference, though," Kundo said. "Deep down."

"I thought so. But there comes a point when you can't trust your own brain, Kundo. My time is gone, but I can't bow out gracefully. I'm full of regrets. I'm full of hate." Hafez bared his teeth and looked like the old Tiger for a minute. "I'm not your wise old grandfather yet, sitting on his balcony playing with the kids. I still want to be *the man,* I want to *matter.* So get to it."

Kundo recounted his entire story and came out of it feeling pathetic and inadequate. He could almost physically feel Hafez's scorn. He doubted the Tiger had ever pined after a lost love.

"You think I'm a fool," Kundo said. He wondered that this old man, literally shaking to bits in front of him, could still make him feel completely inadequate.

"You're definitely a fool," Hafez said. "Why chase after runaway love?"

"I have to know why. Can you understand that? She was literally the only person who gave a shit about me. I have no one else, Hafez. I might as well disappear myself. I have to know how it ended, that she's all right. I keep picturing her dead in a ditch somewhere, or hooked up to some gaming rig, wasting away."

"People make bad choices all the time, Kundo," Hafez said. "This life we have is not that great. Sometimes the relationships you make in virtuality are better. You might not like the answers you find in the end."

Kundo shrugged. "I have to try."

"It's your dime. I'm just the hired gun." Hafez slopped some more whiskey on the bar, but managed to get a fair amount into his mouth. He sighed with satisfaction and used his silk handkerchief to mop up.

The only hired gun I can afford is a senile asshole who literally can't stand straight. I'm doomed.

"I know *Black Road*, of course," Hafez said. "They've been running that racket for the last ten years."

"Who?"

"Satanists? Djinns? I don't know. They keep up a reputation of that black-magic shit, but that's just for the gullible sheep. There's supposed to be a magic city at the end of the road, Gangaridai, the first city of man, removed from this world by the djinn. Paradise. Heaven. Same shit.

"I always thought it was a body racket, you know, jack some matherchods, stick a virus in them, and sell them to some city desperate for nanotech zombies," Hafez said. "Game junkies are great for this, especially now they've got the equipment to go under indefinitely. It's a hoax, man, a scam. Trafficking is the game, flesh peddling. It's the oldest racket in the world. Never goes away, you know that? As long as there's one poor fucker alive with an ounce of work left in him, some rich fucker is going to try and sell him."

"And the city? Ganga . . ."

"Gangaridai." Hafez smiled. "You don't know your history, boy. It's the fabled first city of Bengal, the greatest city every built. People say the djinn ruled it, and when they didn't like the way things were going, they took it away. Fairy stories."

"Took it away where?"

"Somewhere outside of this world. It's a djinn story, you can't take it literally."

"You think Hassem would fall for that?"

"Hmmm, that's the sticking point. That was a canny motherfucker, that hacker of yours. I have a thought. He was investigating your wife, you said."

"Yeah."

"So maybe he fell in love with her and followed her," Hafez said. "Fat motherfucker like that, living in the dark, bound to get obsessed with a pretty woman. Maybe she ticked all his boxes. You ever thought of that?"

"Exactly how many people is she supposed to have run away with?" Kundo asked, exasperated.

Hafez shrugged. "You'd be surprised, man."

Unbidden now, of course, came images of Hassem and her, frolicking in water; for some reason, he always saw the hacker as an aquatic creature. Jealousy had burnt through his neurons too many times in the past years, and now he found this fresh outrage lukewarm, even as he probed at it like a painful tooth. He remembered how she loved to swim, once upon a time. She used to do laps every day at the apartment pool, with her almost militant front crawl, far outpacing him the few times he had accompanied her. When had she stopped swimming? He had never asked her why. Sometimes a deep yearning hit him to go back in time, revisit innocuous interactions with fresh eyes.

"Find the hacker, find your wife," Hafez said. "Don't be alarmed if you find them together. . . ."

Asshole.

"The *Black Road* is the only solid lead we have. Everyone swears that if you go far enough, you win something big," Kundo said. "We have the link on Hassem's rig. He bought a centipede off your nephew just to play one game. We started to play, we won the first two. But one loss and you're out. How do we get far enough on the *Black Road* to get to the city?"

"We?"

"Fara . . . Hassem's neighbor. She's helping me." Kundo held up his hand. "Before you start, it's not romantic. I'm not a gamer, she knows how to play. But she's not that great . . . if she gets knocked out of the tournament we're back to zero."

"So we have to cheat," Hafez said.

"How?"

"I know the greatest cheater of all." Hafez smiled. "Dead Gola."

"Odd name."

"Called that because she cheated death itself."

Chapter Twelve

Dead Gola

They flagged an autopiloted drone taxi. It was a simple box that moved through the air in predetermined paths, as if on invisible rails. The ride was practically free, a few fractions of karma points. The seats were torn and repaired with cheap glue, the insides festooned with faded graffiti. The city fleet was both aging and underused; as more people were driven underground, there was less incentive for Karma to replace her city superstructure.

"I'm being watched," Hafez said, glancing toward the sky before climbing in. "Fucking Karma. I'm on a list. We'll be followed. Fuck it. Can't be helped. Hopefully she'll lose interest."

Kundo felt a surge of pity for the man. *You're not the Tiger anymore, Hafez. I don't think anyone is watching you. Even revolutionaries become irrelevant.*

Kundo helped Hafez in, letting the man have the forward-facing seat. They lifted off with a rattle, and there was a herky-jerky flight path that Kundo followed on his

Echo. He hardly ever took air-cabs, but it was clear that Hafez could not walk for long. They were going deep into the red zone near the river, a part of the city that had been abandoned several years ago. The disembodied voice of the cab tried to dissuade them from entering this area with increasing desperation, even going so far as to promise them a variety of alternate locations where illicit goods and services could be obtained.

Hafez was not doing too well, overcome with tremors and a noticeable slur. Their desultory conversation ceased altogether as Kundo helplessly watched him struggle to find two coherent words. He finally took out a little case, extracted a dermal patch with trembling fingers, and slapped it on the back of his neck. His body seemed to relax and some of the alertness returned to his eyes.

"It happens." Hafez patted the case. "Echo fritzes. Slap one of these on me if you need me sharp."

"What is it?"

"Speed cocktail, basically. Takes a few days off my life every time I use it. Don't frown, Kundo, I'm not trying to live forever here."

The cab air meter was now red and they were running into rough neighborhoods where gangs of camo-swathed men and women watched them with silent hostility. This place was given over wholly to feral zeros, a term coined for those people who had no stake in the city and no faith in the karma-point economy, people who had essentially given up. Karma still fed them and tried to provide basic necessities, and to extract microclime nanites from their bodies in repayment, a system that pleased neither party. The neighborhood here was underwater, a dirty gray tide, a finger stretched out by the Bay of Bengal to probe for weakness.

For an exorbitant fee the air-cab agreed to hover in space for half an hour. Kundo helped Hafez out of the cab into ankle-deep water, wincing as the Tiger's fancy shoes got waterlogged. The seals of his own boots held, mercifully.

The Tiger spent a long minute getting his bearings, and then indicated an abandoned-looking building with illegal plants growing on the roof, someone's version of a kitchen garden. Some of the local wildlife, meanwhile, sloshed toward them, scabs, so called because of their rust-colored hazmat suits and their tendency to use edged weapons. There were scabs in all the abandoned neighborhoods, gangs who ran the streets and salvaged whatever they could.

Hafez pulled out an expensive-looking oblong piece of polished metal from his inner jacket pocket. He thumbed something and it whirred into life, unhinging like an insect, transforming into a snub-nosed, large-bore gun. As the men ambled closer, Hafez calmly unbuttoned his vest, to reveal an *actual bandolier* slotted with very large red bullets. He took one and fed it into the gun, where it settled into the chamber with a satisfying click.

"Depleted uranium slugs," he said loudly. "This here is a war crime." He stared them down like a cowboy. His hand was perfectly steady now, as if the gun had calmed whatever disease ravaged his nerves.

The men took a good look at him and stopped at twenty meters.

"That's a fucking gun," the leading scab said.

"He won't shoot. Look at him. He's fucking geriatric," said the peanut gallery. They were bunched up behind the leading man, however, taking no chances on an errant shot.

"I've got Alzheimer's," Hafez said. "My finger might slip any moment."

"It's only one bullet," the scab said. "Three of us."

"So I'll shoot *you*," Hafez said. "You won't care what I do to your friends. Because you'll be dead."

"I'm gonna gut you, old man." The scab had a vibrating knife in his hand.

"Let's find out if you can."

There was a tense moment as the scab balled up on his feet, deciding.

In the end he did not, in fact, want to find out. Kundo

could only watch with admiration as Hafez's stare broke him completely, and they slunk away with muttered threats of next time.

Even half-dead he's a hundred times more menacing than me. I'm actually jealous of him.

Hafez put the gun away. He was sweating now, abruptly old. Whatever chameleon power he had left was gone for now.

They found the doorway, raised high on steps just a foot above the current waterline. The entrance hall smelled of piss, booze, and some kind of industrial disinfectant. In one corner someone had erected a big tentlike structure. A pair of booted feet were sticking out, accompanied by a raucous snoring that indicated something dire happening in the sleeper's nasal passage.

Hafez whacked his cane across the boots.

"What the fuck, man?" came a muffled voice from inside the tent.

"Wake up, matherchod, it's Hafez."

"Whaaa?"

A disheveled long-haired face emerged, eyes red and squinty, wide-cheekboned face slightly yellowed, all signs of the habitual sygnal user, the best possible drug for the homeless, insofar as it wasn't a drug at all. Sygnal was a little scarab-shaped chip that rode your spine and lit up your brain all day long, no fuss, no organic mess.

"Dead Gola," Hafez said. "Meet Kundo."

Kundo knelt before her. Up close he saw that she was short and powerful-looking, with a machete tied to her left wrist. She smelled of chemicals and sweat and, oddly, of soap.

"You gonna pay?" she asked Hafez, ignoring Kundo.

The old man nodded.

Her face brightened up and she scooted out of her tent and settled into a cross-legged slouch.

"Do you know the game *Final Fantasy*?" Kundo asked.

Gola stared at Kundo with a glimmer of interest.

"I used to code for it."

Kundo looked at her skeptically.

"Fuck off," she said without heat. "What you think I get paid for? Giving blowjobs?"

"There's a game called *Black Road*."

"Ah."

"You know it."

"Sure." Gola smiled. "You ain't the first guy coming to me for help."

"Who?" Kundo blinked a picture of Hassem over to the coder's Echo. "This guy?"

"Yup. Good old Hassem."

"You knew him?"

"Sure. Back when I was a flash coder. Knew everyone. Guess how many people I knew when I got fired? Zero."

Gola shrugged. She didn't seem that bothered by this apparent mass exodus of friends. There was an insouciant cheerfulness about her that was endearing.

Kundo felt a rush of sympathy for her. "What happened to you then?"

Something in his face must have resonated, because Gola seemed to dampen her natural reflex to tell him to fuck off and actually decided to answer.

"Sygnal junky," she said, tapping her scarab. "Was from the beginning. Square Enix never gave a shit before but new management came in. Wanted a cleanup. Clean coders? You kidding me? Anyway, old story. They let me go about five years ago. I had a good severance but guess what, it came to about, let's see . . . four and a half years of a steady supply of sygnal. You give a junky a pile of cash, what you think is gonna happen?"

"You didn't get another job?"

"I was so fried every day it didn't even occur to me. Thought the KP would last forever. Lost touch with everyone, of course. Sygnal does that. It ain't a social drug. No passing around the peace pipe and shit. Ended up here when Karma pretty much erased me from her systems."

"She can do that?"

Gola laughed. "Well, thing is, I died. Like, legit: my heart stopped and PMD went off-line. My dealer brought me back with some illegal defib software, but I think it busted something in the PMD 'cause now Karma thinks I'm dead. Hahaha."

"Karma thinks you're dead. . . ."

"I'm a ghost," Gola said. She made a fluttering motion with her short fingers.

"Useful," Hafez said. "To be dead. Dead Gola is a legend."

"Yeah," Gola said. "Some people want some black shit done only dead people can do. That's when they use me."

"Like what?"

Gola shrugged, glanced at Hafez. "We ain't saints."

"What did you do for Hassem?" Kundo asked.

"Some dark shit, on and off. Corpsing. You know what that is? Guys pay to have their Echos linked up with a bunch of dead bodies. It's gotta be fresh bodies, before the Echo decomposes."

"What for?"

"To fuck 'em, what do you think? You can make 'em move around if you're strong enough."

"Hassem?"

"He wanted to be a necromancer. Kept talking about lich kings and shit. Anyway, that was before he became a Road-head. Guy became obsessed easily."

Tell me about it. Hassem, you sick fuck, I wish I'd never hired you.

"Last thing I did for him was pretty harmless. There are some old glitches in *FF9000*," Gola said. "There's always some dickless noob who wants an easy way. Never understood how he became a Black Roader, but he got in deep. He had a chart for every player, win ratios, weapons, that sort of shit. Problem was, he was shit at gaming, other than that retro Mario Kart crap he was always going on about. Anyway, I taught him how to win matches."

"Do you know where he is?" Kundo asked, feeling a rush of hope.

"Don't know and don't care," Gola said. "He gave me a month of sygnal and I fucked off."

"He's missing," Kundo said. *Along with my wife.*

"Yeah, lots of people go missing," Gola said. "I heard about that devil's-game shit. Know what I think? Massive hype job. Guerilla marketing for *Black Road,* make the gamers jizz. Who knows, maybe it's a zombie-jacking scam. They got that fat fuck stashed in a basement somewhere getting farmed for nanotech. Karma's a bitch, hahahaha."

"That's exactly what I said." Hafez snorted. "Clean up, Gola, you're coming with us."

"One month sygnal," she said. "You pay same as Hassem. And those are *friend's rates.*"

Hafez just nodded. "Clean up."

Gola got up, grabbed a gym bag from her tent, and disappeared deeper into the building. Kundo cringed at the thought of bringing her to Fara's apartment, but half an hour later he found that she did, in fact, clean up fairly well. Somewhere in the bowels of the structure was a working bathroom and shower, because she returned in a rumpled but clean tracksuit, wet hair slicked back, and a black scarf to cover her head and face. The machete was sheathed discreetly against her thigh. She smelled strongly of soap now.

He stared at her incredulously. There was a rough attractiveness about her. She looked great.

"I'm not an animal you know," she said with a smirk. "Just dead and homeless."

Chapter Thirteen

Mixed Sygnals

Kundo took one look at Fara's face and quickly realized that he had been far too blasé about bringing Dead Gola into the premises. They shuffled miserably into her cramped living room, while she stood in her kitchen and glared unrelentingly at Kundo. Worse, Sophy attached herself firmly to Dead Gola, happily hugging the former coder's leg. Kundo saw Sophy touch the machete and winced. He could almost see the smoke coming out of Fara's ears.

"A. Word. Please. Kundo," she said.

Hafez held out his hand and forestalled him. "Let me."

The old man straightened and approached her with some of his former élan. She stuck out her hand in a militant gesture, but Hafez was well practiced at turning hostile ladies, and before she knew it, he had flipped her wrist and was kissing her knuckles. His accompanying words, murmured just below earshot, must have also been charming, because Fara lost her froideur completely. Kundo watched, irritated, as she smiled, then *giggled,* and finally linked arms with Hafez and led him to the best chair in the house, as if he were a lord or something.

The Tiger winked at him.

"Gola, meet the lady of the house," Hafez said with a bow. "Our most gracious hostess."

"Welcome, all of you." For some reason she was still giving him a black look. "Some tea? Kundo, come with me next door for a moment, Hashem's machine is much better."

She grabbed his arm the second they were outside, fingernails digging into his skin.

"Are you *insane*? Bringing a sygnal junkie over?"

"She's no—"

"Don't even say it!" Fara hissed. "I can see the scab on her neck a mile away. She's *twitchy,* Kundo! Do you even know what happens to sygnal junkies on a fucking regular basis?"

"Um . . ."

"They fucking have fits where they puke and piss and shit themselves, Kundo! I've got two living in the floor below me."

"She worked on the game," Kundo said with his best non-offensive calming voice.

This seemed to further infuriate Fara.

"She's going to stay in Hassem's apartment. Hafez, too. You're going to sleep on my couch and if she tries to break into my place you're going to handle that," Fara said. "You're really just going to bring two complete strangers here and expect me to put them up? With Sophy?"

"I didn't think."

"Yeah." A last withering look. "I'm beginning to see your fucking problem."

That night Dead Gola duly complied, suffering a complete breakdown. Kundo woke up to a polite but determined knocking. Terrified of Sophy waking up, he stumbled to the door, and found Hafez in a dark-green silk dressing gown, hair combed back perfectly, eyes a bit wild. There was a fresh speed patch on his neck.

"Come. Gola is ill."

She was sprawled across Hassem's play couch, body stiff and shaking, fingers and toes curled. Kundo went to reach for her and then stopped short when he saw she was covered in copious amounts of vomit. Her pants were already soaked with piss. The smell was so thick he could almost taste it. He looked around, feeling like a coward, unable to take a step further into that miasma of bodily fluids. *I'm just the worst shit in the world. She's probably dying and I'm scared of getting my hands dirty.*

"For god's sake, Kundo, help me!" Hafez yelled. He was cradling her head on his knee. "Get her mouth open and put in my belt. My fingers are shaking too much. She's going to bite through her tongue soon."

He found that being yelled at was beneficial in such a crisis, the simple directions a great relief. He ignored the wetness of the couch and pried open her mouth, forcing the belt between her teeth, repressing a slight shudder as he touched her. The sygnal scarab was gleaming black against her muscular neck. He made to take it off, but Hafez stopped him.

"She'll go into a seizure if you do that."

"This *isn't* a seizure?"

"It'll be worse. Her PMD doesn't work properly. Her heart might stop."

"Hospital," Kundo said. *God, please let her die anywhere but here,* he thought and then felt immediately like a shit.

"Can't," Hafez said impatiently. He was nursing his words, worried about the hit of speed running out. "She's dead, Kundo. Karma won't let her in."

"What do we do, then? Do you know?"

"Sygnal OD is easy. Just keep her from choking, keep the fever down, and let her ride it out. We need to tie her up so she doesn't thrash around and hurt herself." Hafez looked around the dark room with faint disgust. "You better find something. This damn place is like a cave."

Kundo found the linen cupboard, which had a collection of towels and sheets, even though Hassem did not own a conventional bed. Everything was old and moldy-smelling, the vestiges of long-ago parental concern, perhaps. He tore some sheets into strips and returned. They tied Gola down as best as they could. Hafez was ashen, his movements already jerky and graceless.

"You rest," Kundo said, scared that Hafez himself would collapse. "I've got her."

"Keep the head sideways," Hafez said. "Don't let her thrash around, she'll snap her neck."

Kundo wet some towels with disinfectant and started cleaning her up, wiping the couch down as best he could. He considered changing her clothes but that seemed too much of a liberty to take with someone he had just met, not least because she was the type of person who kept a machete tied to her wrist. He settled for blotting her wet clothes as much as possible and then spraying her with disinfectant to get rid of the worst of the smell. He wrapped a towel around her waist for good measure. His nose was dead by now anyway, but he knew the entire place must reek.

He resisted the urge to change out of his own clothes, figuring that Gola might release further bodily fluids in the near future. He finally sat at her head, trying to imitate Hafez's pose.

She went into routine fits, severe enough to arc her spine completely off the couch, the corded muscles of her neck bulging with frightening intensity. Kundo hugged her tight in those moments, straining against her immense drug-fueled strength. The rest of the time he wiped her brow with a wet cloth. Fever raged through her, and after a few hours the fits tailed off in intensity, her body exhausted.

She was parched, so Kundo dribbled water across her cracked lips, loath to wake up Hafez, who was himself in a shallow, restless sleep. He had never nursed anyone before and fretted in constant fear of somehow breaking his patient. More than once he almost pinged Fara, but suffering alone seemed preferable to her scorching commentary.

By sunrise the worst was over and he was able to doze off, Gola's head on his lap, both of them plastered with sweat but otherwise whole. Fara woke him up with an uncharacteristically gentle shake.

"It happened then," she said.

"Yes." Kundo avoided her gazed.

"Why didn't you wake me up, Kundo? I could have helped."

Kundo shrugged. "I thought you'd be mad."

"Yes, Kundo," Fara said. "But I would have helped. God, you're a moron sometimes. Just . . . just call me next time, okay? We're a team."

Kundo looked around. "All of us? Some team. I've added a sygnal junkie and a geriatric lothario who can't string together two sentences without slapping on a speed patch."

Fara looked at him sadly. "We're all that's left, Kundo. Maybe this is all there is. You don't even know her and you stayed up all night holding her head."

Kundo looked down. "She can't go to hospital."

"That's not what I meant," Fara said.

Chapter Fourteen

Cheaters Always Win

Dealing with Gola was much easier in the morning. Hafez was at his best during the day, more than capable of directing traffic, and with Fara's help they were able to get her bathed, changed, and fed with some kind of broth. She improved steadily and said a few words in between bouts of sleeping. When he was well rested, Hafez made them laugh with stories of the many different kinds of drug fits he had dealt with, and other times Fara played music for them on Hassem's system.

Hassem's apartment, foreboding and alien, became more human almost imperceptibly. An assortment of blankets and pillows now adorned the various couches, and Hafez had somehow rigged the lights so the place lost the weird blue glow and instead offered warmer hues. There was no dining table, so they took their meals on the floor in a circle, sitting cross-legged, an activity Sophy found hilarious. They ate rice and potatoes fried with onions from Hassem's vat kitchen.

Hafez, used to finer fare, insisted on trying to make some egg concoction, which ended in sorrow and mirth, an inedible mess that smelled of kerosene. Sophy used it to make slop castles, until her mother made her throw it away.

"In the old town, there are kitchens that make real food," Hafez said. "Secret places where you get real fish and live chickens. You don't know how good actual food tastes."

"That's disgusting," Kundo said. He looked around. It felt good to eat with other people. Even Dead Gola's snuffling was oddly companionable.

By evening she was conscious and sitting up, acutely embarrassed, apologizing disjointedly every few minutes. Her voice was hoarse from the vomiting. Kundo, who had repeatedly wished her elsewhere throughout the night, now found himself robbed of any ill will. He discovered that having nursed her he was imbued with a hazy sort of affection for her. Fara apparently felt the same way, because in the middle of the tenth spluttered apology she wrapped Gola in an enormous hug, whereupon the hacker smiled and shut up.

"That was sweet of you," Kundo said later, when they were clearing away dinner.

"I *am* a sweet person," Fara said.

"Since when, exactly?" Kundo smiled and then quickly

held up his hands in surrender as her face elongated into a pre-shout rictus.

Gola had pointedly removed her spent sygnal patch and not yet replaced it with a fresh one, which Kundo knew she had an ample supply of, having himself emptied her pockets and boxed her belongings. Aside from the bundle of sygnal patches, there was chewing gum; a pocket knife; a little palmtop computer device; some kind of headache medication; a Twix bar; a card of satellite minutes, which was often used as black-market currency; and bits of paper on which she had written contact info by hand, perhaps not trusting her Echo. And the machete, of course. Kundo silently handed her the box, considering that this was possibly the sum of her life, these few things.

"Not much, is it?" Gola said, reading his expression. "For a life."

Kundo shrugged. Now that she was awake he felt terribly clumsy, as if he could damage her with any ill-advised word. As usual he found himself tongue-tied and uncertain.

"So you're doing all this to find your wife, huh?"

"It started off like that," Kundo said. "Seems like it's a little bit bigger now."

"She must have been something special."

Kundo shrugged. "She was to me. I thought so. Everyone is special to someone, right?"

I think I broke her somehow. No. She broke on her own somehow and I just ignored it. And now what am I doing? Trying to turn back the clock? To make amends?

"Not everyone," Gola said. "You're a famous artist. I looked you up."

"I was, I guess."

"I thought you'd live in a fuck-off mansion." Gola looked around. "Not this dump. No offense."

Kundo thought about it. "I do have a better address. But I prefer living here, I suppose. Too many bad memories at the old place. It made me crazy, every little thing just pointing out my losses. I would pick up a cup or a book and it would just hit me with sadness and anger and failure."

"What about all your painting stuff?" Gola asked.

"I haven't painted in three years," Kundo said. Strangely, he didn't mind her asking, but how could he really explain that blank canvasses haunted him with guilt and anxiety, that the mere sight of one made his stomach fall and his heart beat uncomfortably fast? "I can't."

"I used to live for coding, you know?" Gola said. "I get it, man."

"Do you miss your old life?" Kundo asked.

"I can't really differentiate between old and new. I

mean, I know it looks like two lives from the outside. I was Gola the star tech, and then I was Dead Gola the homeless junkie, fucking for sygnal. But I don't know if that was ever really two different lives. I can't explain it properly. I mean from the inside, it feels like I've just kept doing the same things and it's the world that changed around me."

I know exactly what you mean. Everything is fine until it becomes alien one day and we realize that we didn't really get instructions on how to live at all, and all our little life hacks don't work anymore.

He wanted to hug her but settled for patting her shoulder awkwardly and then wincing at his own inadequacy. He would have sent her an emoji, a burst of psychic warmth, but her Echo did not work; she was cut off from the world in a far crueler way than he had fully plumbed. He was relieved when Fara and Hafez came over.

"You ready to cheat yet?" Hafez asked.

"The hack is old," she said, rummaging through her own stuff. "So old that actually only a handful of people even have the gear to do it."

"But Hassem used the centipede."

Gola took her pocketknife and started tinkering around with the couch. Eventually she connected a PS4 controller, one of Hassem's museum-piece artifacts, to the couch with a cable.

"The FF game is very old. They don't rewrite all the code from scratch for these games, they just build on top. Some of the code goes back to the time people used physical controllers to move their characters around the screen," Gola said. "There was an old hack in the game that never got patched, because everything switched to VR shortly after. Before Echo or VR, people used to play games using these controllers and watch the action on television screens."

She pulled up the game on the little viewing screen on the couch and did some button-mashing, which brought up the *Final Fantasy* main menu with its operatic score.

"I taught Hassem how to rig this," Gola said. "I'm going to walk you through it. You have to do it while you're in the couch, right before you go under. There's a specific timing. First you select a random person's game session with the Join button, but don't actually join. This is just setting up the PS button double tap, which takes you to your previous screen very quickly. Then you sit on your horse and open your inventory and during the lag you quickly double tap the PS button to take you to your previous screen, which is the random person's game session. You click Join, but when it asks you if you're sure, you cancel out. This glitches out the game. A gray screen should pop up that looks like you've crashed the game, but you really haven't. At that moment you're glitched but you can still access some options. The first thing to do is put on your invincible armor. You won't be able to see the inventory screen, so it has to be the only item available in your armor slot and you have to remember the keys to get there. Then you have to kill yourself. The Easy Way Out option is 'Right, L2, Down, R1, Left, Left, R1, L1, L2, L1'* on this PS4 controller. It used to be a default option in an old version of the game, and the code is still there, but of course no one uses physical controllers anymore."

"Okay," Fara said. "And after I die?"

"You respawn in the game in free roam and you can enter the death match, but you're still glitched out. It looks like you're naked, but actually you're wearing the invincible armor. You won't be able to wear anything else, of course, but the death match itself won't realize you've got illegal armor."

"So I'm going to fight naked?" Fara asked.

"Yes, a few people do that anyway, since the armor in the death match is bog-standard crap and you get a speed bonus if you're naked," Gola said.

Fara winced. "I'm going to be really uncomfortable doing that."

---

* Actually this is from *Grand Theft Auto: San Andreas*. *Final Fantasy 9000* is an amalgamation of *GTA, Red Dead,* and *Final Fantasy*.

Gola laughed. "You guys have just spent the past twenty-four hours cleaning up my piss and vomit. I'm pretty sure one of you wiped my ass and gave me a sponge bath. You're seriously worried about your *avatar* being naked?"

"Can't you do the glitch?" Fara asked.

"I'm dead, the game won't even recognize my Echo," Gola said. "Funny, right? Coder who can't game."

"I have Alzheimer's," Hafez said. He tapped the side of his head. "Probably give me a seizure."

"I'm going to end up stabbing myself in the first minute," Kundo said.

"Fine, you shits," Fara said. "So what happens if it works?"

"Then you fight the death match normally, using the couch. You should be slick as shit, with the centipede and the naked bonus on top. Of course, when you do get hit, you'll only take a tiny bit of damage."

"There's only one problem," Fara said. "I don't have any invincible armor."

"So it's actually just grade-S specialized armor, it can be of any class, either heavy, middle, or light," Gola said. "Mithril armor absorbs the most damage, Vulpine armor poisons the enemy every time he hits you, and Chocobo feather armor ramps up your evasion to an insane level, where enemy blows just pretty much glide off you."

"Yeah, I don't have any of those. People grind years to get one set," Fara said.

"Hassem had the Chocobo," Gola said. "He bought it on the dark Web."

"That's great for him."

"We can transfer it to you," Gola said. "If you know how to get into his account. What's his security apparatus?"

"It's all breath-controlled," Kundo said.

Gola whistled and made a pricey motion with her fingers. "Flash motherfucker."

"It's actually set to her breath as well," Kundo said.

Gola raised an eyebrow. Fara's face darkened perceptibly.

"Problem solved, then," Gola said. "Lucky guy."

"It's not . . . we were just friends," Fara said. "He was a little obsessed with me, maybe. Kundo found a bunch of feeds. . . . Well. If you find nudes and shit of me floating around his system, it wasn't me giving them to him."

Gola smiled at her. "Hey, you don't have to explain, okay? I'd be obsessed with you, too, if you were my neighbor."

She got Fara to breathe on the console and started fiddling with it again.

What the hell is Gola leering at her for? Oh . . . um, she's hitting on her. Well, this is awkward. Fara's got that giggle again. She did that with the geriatric lothario Hafez, too. Does Fara giggle whenever anyone hits on her? She's never giggled at me. This is ridiculous. Gola just got out of a damn coma and is already flirting. What a beast. I better warn Fara. She probably doesn't even know what's going on. Who am I kidding? She's totally turning red.

He watched them laughing, huddled around the centipede couch, Sophy toddling between their legs like an excited pup, and felt a pang of melancholy, as if he were outside them, a pathetic invisible creature gnawing at the surface of the earth unable to burrow in. *These broken people just met, how are they able to settle into this rhythm, as if they were always meant to be together at this very moment? What do I lack, then? Does my artist's eye make me this way, condemned to watch? I am a mirror, cold and lifeless, returning only a pale copy of what is given to me. What is it like to be my companion? Is it worse than being alone?*

Sophy, bless her, thought he was part of the circle, and when she was tired she plopped down in his lap and hit him several times with her pudgy fists, having decided some time ago that he was her mock nemesis, play monster, and all-round punching bag. There was much hilarity when she got him on the nose, and as an involuntarily tear streamed from his eye even Sophy was temporarily concerned and tried to blow on it in an imitation of her mother's own ministrations to minor wounds.

He hushed Sophy and kept her still in his lap, breathing in the baby smell that still came from the top of her head. Holding Sophy was always bittersweet. It made him think of the children he could have had, the child he had once refused. It haunted him, the possibility that his wife might have silently pined for one, as he was doing now. Then he felt like a shit for not loving Sophy more. *There's a child right here, whom I could love . . . and yet I cannot, I want my own, I think only of my own flesh and blood, my own fictitious family. This whole stupid myth of passing on your genes, making little copies of yourself, racking us with guilt.*

"We can start now," Gola said finally.

They turned their backs to let Fara slather herself in gel in private. The glitch required her to be half-in, half-out of the centipede's embrace, using the controller manually. Even with Gola standing beside her, it took twelve tries before it worked. Everyone cheered when the naked witch avatar finally flickered into the small screen. Fara gave them a thumbs-up as she dropped the controller and relaxed into the couch.

Her avatar sparked into life on the road, and almost instantly settled into a match, armed with talwar and shield and nothing else, her Chocobo armor invisible, of course. The anatomy was remarkably lifelike and drew smirks from both Gola and Hafez. Kundo could almost see Fara cringing inside the worm embrace of the couch.

Her movement was now noticeably faster, both from the naked speed bonus as well as the evasion bonus of the Chocobo armor. The first match came and ended fast, Fara dodging the first blow, dancing past the guard, and then stabbing the enemy through the back of the neck.

She won seven more battles in quick succession, against opponents ranked far higher than her. Chocobo armor could only be defeated with special weapons and spells, none of which were permitted in the death match. She could feel their rage as one by one they realized she was cheating, but the whole tournament was underground; there was no one to complain to. *FF9000* admins did not even know this map was being sponsored by a third party.

The ninth battle was against a well-known player called LordNelson, known chiefly for amassing a huge fortune in game money in the briefly popular cowboy game *Red Dead Redemption 9000* over ten years ago. As far as the Echosphere knew, he had never played *Final Fantasy* officially, and, in fact, had publicly ranted that all sword and sorcery–type games were regressive and preventing gaming culture from evolving to the next step.

The chief problem was that LordNelson also walked onto the road naked, and after the first exchange it was clear that he was packing something extra.

"He's not taking damage, Gola!" Fara's voice was shrill through the couch speakers.

"I can see that," Gola said through gritted teeth. She elbowed Kundo and Hafez out of the way and sat squarely in front of the screen, controller in hand. "Your health went down a bit!"

"How? He didn't even touch me!"

"The fucker is wearing Vulpine armor!"

"What do I do? What do I do?"

"Dodge for now!"

"That's what I'm fucking doing!" Fara shouted.

"Don't hit him, you'll only get poisoned!"

"Stop yelling at me!"

"Okay, okay, everyone calm down," Gola said. She glared at Kundo for no reason.

"Do something," Hafez said. "She's going to lose."

"He's a hacker, just like us," Gola said. "He's using the same exact glitch."

"So what happens now? The game just times out?"

"Yeah, eventually," Gola said. "But you're gonna lose because you're poisoned." She connected her palmtop computer into another little jack in the couch. A cheap hologram screen and keyboard popped out of each end of the little black box. "I can stop him, though. Let's see . . . nope. Um, nope. Shit, I can't actually do much." Lines of code were running across the screen, and her stubby fingers were racing across the virtual keyboard. Kundo stared in fascination. He had never seen anyone type this fast before. It was a long-defunct skill.

"Gola, earn your fucking keep," Hafez said under his breath. Even shaking to bits, he was still gangster to his core.

"Hang on, hang on," Gola said.

"Okay, Fara?" Gola said.

"Yeah!"

"Listen up. The best I can do is run a batch file that's going to reset both of you. Deglitch you, essentially," Gola said. "You'll lose your armor but so will he. You'll be really naked."

"How's that gonna help me?"

"Well, you'll know exactly when you're deglitched. He won't. You gotta take advantage. Best I can do."

"You think I can beat him?" Fara asked doubtfully.

Gola shrugged. "He's not that great at sword fighting, either. Used to play cowboy games, remember? You got a fair shot."

"Okay."

"So get a good position and tell me when. You'll get one free hit before he figures it out. Make it count."

"Yup."

"Ready?"

"Wait. Wait. Waaaaiiiit. Now! Now! Now!"

Fara closed her eyes and attacked with reckless abandon. She went instinctively low, a fencer's thrust to the under-belly, and it hit flush, tearing up entrails and angling into the chest cavity. The Vulpine armor winked out and his face crumpled in shock and then agony, as whatever rig he was using abruptly flooded his pain receptors. Hardened gamers played at half-mast with the pain dial; it was considered bad form to have it much below 25 percent, a toddler's option, the coward's way out; an impromptu evisceration wasn't great even at a quarter rate. Blood splattered Fara's face and there was a long moment of thrashing about before the game decided that LordNelson would not recover. His cryptic shriek of "Oh my god, they killed Kenny!" was the last thing they heard.

As usual, the characters faded from view and every-thing turned black, except this time a set of numbers flashed on-screen for a couple of seconds, gone before their eyes had even properly registered it.

"What was that?" Kundo asked, scrambling to write it down.

"It's gone! I remember the first three digits. . . ." Fara said. She was halfway out of the couch, ripping off the centipedes, flinging bits of blue gel all over the place.

"Calm down," Gola said. She had her nose to the little screen, her fingers on her pad. "I can still see the afterim-age. Okay. Got it."

Kundo helped Fara out of the couch and wrapped her in a thick towel robe. Her eyes were manic with excitement.

"We won! We won we won we won!" Fara gathered them into a giant hug, and even Hafez didn't mind getting blue gunk all over his silk dressing gown.

Kundo felt Gola stiffen in their collective embrace, but then she started to laugh and so did everyone else and for a moment it felt like they had really won something.

Chapter Fifteen

A Curious Visitor

Kundo led them next morning to their regular pub in a buoyant mood and the bartender greeted them by name, raising an exaggerated eyebrow at Gola and the Tiger.

"You're multiplying!" he said in mock horror.

"Hafez, at your service." Hafez bowed in turn, and then introduced Dead Gola, who gave him a death stare.

The bartender took things in stride and even complimented the old man on his suit. "Standard, right? One of everything?"

"Double it up, my good man," Kundo said with celebratory zest.

Later, ensconced in the biggest booth, surrounded by hot food and the kind of chatter four excited adults and a toddler can make, Kundo thought that this was not too bad for a Tuesday morning.

"The coordinates are for Tulsi Hills," Fara said, once they had sated their initial hunger pangs. "One of the mansions. Does anyone even live there?"

"Very rich people," Kundo said. "Well, they own the mansions. I don't know if they bother living there anymore."

Then he stopped talking and stared at the door, along with everyone else. The bartender, normally unflappable, froze mid-swipe, his washcloth hovering two inches above the bar. They stared because the door flung open without anyone discernably touching it.

A black-haired young woman with a vaguely gothic air wearing heavy boots clomped in after a theatrical pause, a gold nose ring winking on her face somehow accentuating an overall air of sulkiness. A clumpy cigarette hung from the corner of her mouth. She took a deep puff in blatant disregard of the pub's no-smoking policy, and blew an impossibly large quantity of fragrant air directly at them. The sweet smell of organic weed instantly suffused Kundo's brain, making his eyes water and his throat itch. He suppressed the urge to cough.

"Umm, hello, er, no smoking?" the bartender objected in an oddly high voice.

"Oh, shut up, Rahima," the woman said with venom, whereupon he duly slunk behind his tap and refused to make eye contact with anyone, all the while muttering that his name, in fact, was not Rahima and that he was a boy.

The woman stomped her way over to them and pulled

a chair up to the booth. Her clothes were all various shades of black, some loose, some satiny and tight, the entire ensemble giving off the air of high fashion and angst. This close, Kundo realized that the makeup and nose ring had aged her somewhat; she was, in reality, no more than a teenager.

"I'm RetroKPopGirl, you can call me ReGi. Duchess of Kathmandu."

Marvelous Kathmandu, jewel of the Himalayas, queen of cities, Kundo's Echo went off in a hyperbolic paean.

"I've been there," Kundo said. "I was told the nobility was abolished."

"I was appointed by Karma," ReGi said. "For services rendered. Newly minted duchess, go ahead and check."

"Ah, Karma rules there, too, then," Hafez said. "She's doing a better job in Kathmandu, I hope. We were promised the earth and only got a mouthful of seaweed."

"She's not that bad," ReGi said. "Anyway, she sent me here to help out her sister. All the Karmas are related, did you know that?"

"Why are you here, exactly?" Kundo asked. *Hafez was right. I guess Karma was watching all along.*

"I told you, Kathmandu sent me."

"I mean *here in this pub.*"

She pulled out a five-pointed gold-plated star from a pocket and slapped it down on the table. This caused

Saad Z. Hossain

one of the water bulbs to teeter over, resulting in spillage and a general flurry of mopping, which set Sophy off into paroxysms of giggling.

"Sorry," said ReGi once the chaos had been contained. "Your Karma gave me that. I'm a sheriff!"

She beamed at them, and then seemed utterly disappointed at their blank looks.

"You know, sheriff? Like I ride into town and kick ass?"

"We haven't the foggiest idea, dear child," Hafez said.

"You look like an ass-kicker," ReGi said, looking him over. "An old one. But still. Those clothes aren't fooling me."

Hafez bowed.

"And you," ReGi turned to Gola. "There's something wrong with you. Karma can't see you on her systems."

"I'm dead," Gola said.

"Oh, right. Well, you've got lovely skin."

Gola smiled. "I just came out of a sygnal seizure. These morons made me drink four liters of electrolytes."

"Right? Sygnal is really shit. You know, you should switch to organic weed. I've got just the right supply. . . . Well, never mind, we'll talk later about that." She turned to Fara. "You're the chick with the baby. You're prettier in real life. Karma's cams really add like ten, fifteen pounds on you. . . . But you're, like, kind of delicious-looking."

"Thanks a lot."

"Yeah, hello, baby," ReGi said to Sophy. Sophy reached over and tried to grab the sheriff's star, got poked by the pointy end, and started howling.

"And you're the artist Kundo," ReGi said over the din. "You used to be quite good. I thought you were dead. But here you are, alive and well. . . . It's actually kind of disappointing."

"I haven't painted anything in years," Kundo said. He laughed. "My agent has stopped calling and the gallery has gone out of business altogether. So I guess I might as well be dead."

"Well, that's depressing," ReGi said. "Anyway, what I hear is that the four of you have cracked the game."

"Mmm," Kundo said.

"Which is weird, because you guys are, like, total losers. On paper, I mean."

"Thanks," Kundo said.

"And now you've got a golden ticket to the chocolate factory," ReGi said.

"Yes, you seem to know a lot," Kundo said. "Er, what chocolate factory?"

"Well, I *am* the sheriff," ReGi said. "Sorry, the chocolate factory is an old story. You guys probably don't know it. I collect old stories."

"What exactly do you want with us?" Kundo asked.

"See, I've been sent here to investigate a problem," ReGi said. "There is a place on the map where Karma's surveillance does not work."

"That makes her nervous, I suppose," Hafez said. "A damn sight too much surveillance in this town."

"You're an anarchist, you *would* say that," ReGi said. "Don't worry, I feel the same way, uncle."

"You work for her," Hafez spat. "And don't look at me all googly-eyed, I'm not falling for your uncle crap—"

"I *am not* making googly eyes!" Her eyes, in fact, were glowing an alarming red now.

"This place. Let me guess. It's number four Tulsi Hills," Fara said.

"Bingo."

"Why isn't Karma sending in the drones?" Hafez asked.

"Drones aren't the answer to every problem, uncle," ReGi said.

Hafez snorted. "She wasn't that shy when she cleared the Night Market ten years ago."

"Don't get me wrong," ReGi said. "It's not a moral stance. I mean drones are not likely to work here. Traditional hardware has been proven to be . . . problematic."

"There's something in Tulsi Hills that both resists surveillance and is too powerful for normal weapons?" Kundo asked. "What do you expect us to do? Talk it to death?"

"Investigate," ReGi said. "I want you to do whatever you were planning to do anyway. Go follow the story. Find out what's happening. Let me peek over your shoulder."

"You mean Karma rides our shoulder," Hafez said.

"Yes, well, she's always watching her flock." ReGi took out a box from inside her coat and opened it. Inside were five shiny gold-tinted stars identical to the one she herself carried. "In return, I'm offering to deputize you. Karma's mark. Your ticket to command any service or good within the city bounds or any demesne ruled by *any version of Karma*. You know how many cities have a Karma running shit? You're gold in all of them. You can act as you see fit, follow your story wherever it goes. I even made one for the baby."

Hafez took one in his trembling hand. "I could call in drone strikes with this. . . ."

"Within reason," ReGi said. "Yes."

"My answer is, go fuck yourself," Hafez said.

"Uncle!"

"I took a bullet to the ribs in the Night Market," Hafez said. "Karma killed three thousand people, and the bodies disappeared without a trace. In '82 we got tear-gassed when they shut the port. So, yeah. Fuck Karma and fuck anyone who does her dirty work."

"Go fuck yourself!" Sophy parroted in singsong.

"Hush, baby." Fara covered her ears. "He's right. Fuck

Karma. We've come this far on our own."

ReGi looked sad.

"Sorry, would you like something to eat?" Kundo asked, acutely uncomfortable whenever anyone was upset within his vicinity.

She sniffed. "No, thanks. Rahima will probably spit in my food."

"Er, his name is actually Ron," Kundo said. He looked around awkwardly, and spotted a stack of pancakes so far untouched. "How about these?"

"Thanks." ReGi tucked her joint behind her ear and cut up the pancakes into tiny pieces and drenched them with syrup. She started defiantly cramming them into her mouth.

"Juice?" Kundo asked.

"No."

"Look, perhaps we could have said that a bit differently. . . ." Kundo said.

"I get it, no one likes Karma."

"Well, we didn't mean to upset you."

"I'm *not* upset. I just spent a lot of effort finding out about all of you. You all seemed so nice. It took a lot of time to make those badges."

"Sorry. Of course. We'll wear the badges, won't we, guys? They look sort of cool." Kundo looked around haplessly.

Hafez snorted. "She's playing you, fool."

"Oh, shut up, uncle," ReGi said.

"She checks out," Gola said abruptly. She lifted up her little handheld device. "Lady of the Garden, Kathmandu. Official title. Currently on secondment to Chittagong. That sheriff's badge of hers is no joke. Carte blanche in Chittagong, courtesy of Karma. She could shoot someone on the street and *it'd be legal.*"

"Duh. I told you."

"What I want to know is, why would Kathmandu send a kid to investigate this haunted house or whatever in Tulsi?" Gola asked. "What's so special about you?"

"How rude!"

"She's got a good point," Kundo said apologetically.

"Fine. I'm a djinn."

"What?"

"Djinn. You know. Made of fire, live forever." She wiggled her fingers. "Turn you into frogs with magic. That kind of thing."

"You're a duchess djinn sheriff?" Gola asked. "Like, do you know how insane this is?"

"Well, you're looking for people who have apparently disappeared into a video game run by the devil," ReGi said. "So don't tell me about weirdness."

"Let's say we believe you. This death house in Tulsi," Kundo said. "Djinns?"

"Maybe."

"This game is supposed to be run by the devil," Kundo said. "Horus, the kid said. Is there a djinn by that name?"

"Maybe."

"Get off it," Hafez said. "They've been bandying about the name of Horus on the streets for years now. Guy with a chest like burnt toast, wearing someone else's legs. It's a myth. I'm telling you, there's nothing in that house but a bunch of rich fucks dragging in losers and farming them."

"As I said, Karma cannot look inside," ReGi said. "The only way in is with an invitation."

"So they got tech better than Karma's," Hafez said. He looked to the sky in mock benediction. "Hallelujah. I hope they burn this shit down."

"We have an invitation," Kundo said.

"Right. So, fine, you won't work with Karma. Work with me, then. If everything goes to shit *I'll* be your backup."

Hafez looked extremely skeptical, but Kundo forestalled him.

"You said you've been looking into this house. What do you know about the missing people?"

"As in your wife and Hassem? Plus the gamer crew your wife was screwing?"

Kundo winced. *Yeah, those people.*

"Yeah, they weren't the only ones. There's more than

thirteen hundred people missing."

"What?"

"Yeah, thirteen hundred minimum. Hard to say. Might be closer to three thousand. So you can see why Karma's panicking. Too many losses to ignore."

"Fine. Say you're in," Kundo said. "How, exactly, are you going to help? You said none of Karma's toys work in there."

"Yes. Um. Have you ever been possessed?"

Chapter Sixteen

Djinn Rider

It was like being dunked in ice-cold water, and then being held down through the inevitable struggling, the rush of liquid through mouth and nose, the burning, the panic, the zen acceptance of drowning, the final gulp of oxygen leaching away. It was going through all of that and coming out of the other side and realizing the shit was still not over.

He forced himself to open his eyes. Everything was blurry. The first thing he noticed was the absence of the Echosphere. All those bits of information overlaid on the natural world were gone, the maps and signs and updates they all took for granted. That bundle in his brain was replaced by a gleeful imp, a second consciousness that now rode his mind radiating potency.

"Relax. Don't freak out." ReGi's voice blossomed in his head like a flower, releasing the smell of weed, the sound of water falling in a riotous garden, a general sense of spiky outrage. "This is a friendly possession, dude."

His eyes focused and he saw Fara peering down at him. He was on her couch, supine. It was impossible to move any part of his body: not paralysis, but a great lethargy. He wriggled his fingers and toes and found, to his immense, relief that his body still answered to his will. He realized Fara was holding his right hand in a death grip, her nails digging painful crescents into his palm. He did not feel like letting go.

This is real. I can't believe it. Djinns. I can feel it. She is alien.

"Can you stand up?" Fara asked.

Kundo got up on shaky legs. His feet felt rubbery. He could smell sulfur, but that was probably his imagination.

They stared at him, openmouthed. Sophy pointed and gave a loud shout of laughter.

"What?"

"Kundo! Look!" Fara's eyes were huge.

He looked down. His feet were levitating six inches off the floor. He was floating on air.

"It's real, then." Hafez touched an amulet he wore around his neck, the one with Arabic script of the Ayatul Kursi. "Salaam, djinn. God's peace on you."

Kundo's heartbeat was cannonballs rolling in his chest, as everything clenched in atavistic fear. He staggered to his knees.

"Oh, stop it, you old man, you're perfectly fine," ReGi

said. "I'm the one having an out-of-body experience. . . . God, how do you live in this damn thing? It's so . . . unwieldy."

Kundo looked around wildly, half expecting ReGi's body to be floating around.

"We put her in the centipede," Gola said from the kitchen.

"What?"

"Yeah, it's the perfect place. I mean, it'll keep her clean, comfortable, fully hydrated," Gola said. "Those things can keep you going indefinitely."

Kundo wasn't following. He was shouting in his own head in adrenaline-fueled panic. *So you can read my thoughts? Can you see through my eyes?*

"Everything," ReGi said. "Can you calm down, please? Your PMD is so hot it's going to burn a hole in your spine."

Okay. Okay. I'm possessed. It doesn't feel that bad. I thought there'd be pain.

"We used to do this all the time to humes," ReGi said. "I heard it was a bit harder back in the day. This Echo thing makes it, like, totally much easier. Your brain is already wired to have an extra rider, and everyone hears voices in their head anyway these days."

And can you take over my body if you wished?

"I'm not gonna do that, duh," ReGi said.

A terrible thought occurred to him. *What happens when I go to the bathroom?*

"I can totally turn myself deaf, dumb, and, um, smell-less," ReGi said.

Really?

"No, not really. You honestly think possession is fun?"

He felt Fara touching his shoulder. She manhandled him to the couch with surprising strength.

"You don't feel any different," she said. She ran a hand lightly across his forehead. "No temperature or anything. Are you sure you're possessed?"

"You saw him floating, right?" Hafez asked.

"Karma got some tricks, too," Gola said.

Kundo closed his eyes. It made it easier to talk to the voice in his head. "Is this some kind of trick? Has Karma taken over my Echo?"

ReGi laughed. "So you believe that Karma can take over your mind through the Echo, but you don't believe in djinns. How is that any different from possession?"

It was strange hearing her sarcastic gurgle in his head. Karma public-service announcements were bland. *If you put it like that, then, Karma's possessed us for years.*

He stood up again. It felt easier this time. He could almost feel an equilibrium forming with his djinn rider. Even the squirming embarrassment of having her privy to every corner of his body was subsiding.

"Kundo. Wow. Kundo," ReGi said. "You should really start painting again. You've got a lot of stuff stored up here."

"Stop it." Kundo flinched.

"Sorry."

"I can't paint. Nothing comes out. Forget about it."

"Okay, dude, chill."

"Are we ready to go to the death house?" Hafez said to Kundo. "If you've finished talking to yourself, that is. The invitation might be time-sensitive." His eyes rested on Sophy. "Not all of us, perhaps."

"I'm not leaving her behind," Fara said calmly. "And I'm not sitting this out, either. The invitation is for me. I won the game."

"You want to take a baby to the death house?" Hafez asked.

"Whatever happens, we go together," Fara said. She turned to Kundo, but she was speaking to the djinn. "You said you're good for protection, ReGi. Do you mean that? Can you keep her safe? If shit goes down will you promise to grab her and run?"

Kundo nodded. "We'll both promise to that."

"You're agreeing to this?" Hafez looked disgusted. "You're going to take a child to war?"

"We're going to talk, Hafez," Kundo said. "We're not

going to war. As long as *you* don't start one, it should be fine."

"Tell that to the three thousand missing," Hafez said.

"Gola?" Kundo said. "You sure you want to come?"

Gola looked surprised. "I sort of thought I was part of the crew."

"Yes, you are." He realized that he meant it.

"I mean, you want me along?" she asked shyly.

"Yes," Kundo said. "Yes, I do."

Chapter Seventeen

Head for the Hills

Hafez arranged transport. His last experience in the rickety air-cab had given him a clear idea of Kundo's lax standards. One should arrive in style to a mansion in Tulsi Hills. These things could not be left up to Kundo. They might end up hiking there.

They decided to give Kundo a day to acclimatize to the possession. He went home briefly to take a bath and get his best clothes and a few other odds and ends. He walked around aimlessly for a time, touching his belongings, and then realized that he was, in effect, saying goodbye. He had no desire to return here. The objects he had once treasured had no hold on him now. He was a rover in truth.

He could feel the presence of the djinn in his head, even though she politely kept herself closed off. It was oddly comforting. He had grown used to other people again, and treasured their company.

"I don't think I'll be coming here again," he said finally, packing his case.

"You're not taking your paintings?" ReGi asked. "That's a lot of money you're leaving behind on the walls. 'Specially if you end up dead."

Kundo shrugged. "I can always paint more. Or not. If I die tomorrow feel free to come here and take what you want. You can keep the body."

"You're a morbid motherfucker, Kundo," ReGi said. "I like it."

Early next morning a beautifully maintained car arrived, a last-century low-slung Mercedes that hung a mere foot in the air, more of a hovercraft than a real flying car. It was maroon and long and detailed with chrome, with an actual human chauffeur in the front, dressed in a black leather apron and cap.

Hafez himself wore his best gray suit and cape, everything handmade and silk-lined. The cape was weighted down with an electrified, telescoping cosh. Various explosives were tucked into other hidden pockets. Underneath his jacket he wore his bandolier, despite Kundo's objections that he was, under no circumstances, to shoot depleted uranium slugs at anyone.

The others cleaned up as best they could, but on reflection Kundo noted that they were still on the edge of raggedy, certainly compared to the chauffeur. Gola had a scarab clamped to her neck beneath her collar, nerves perhaps getting the better of her. She glared at Kundo when she caught him staring at it. He gave her an awkward hug. The machete jacked up her sleeve caught the light sometimes like a piece of errant jewelry.

He had never cared for appearances much, protected by the halo of "creative artist," but it was daunting to pull up on the Tulsi Hill compound, an enclave so well protected that under normal circumstances they would not have dreamt of knocking on the gate.

Even the Tiger, despite his bluster, had never been inside Tulsi. His kingdom at its height had not stretched that far. Even during the brutal Night Market riots no zero had breached these lines.

The car took a circuitous route to Tulsi, avoiding pockets of bad air. The city was not organized coherently. Tulsi was surrounded on three sides by orange zones, connected to the city by one main artery. Tulsi Hills denizens had other means of ingress, apparently, for they had allowed this municipal road to fall to ruin.

The last stretch covered a red zone abandoned fully to the zeros, where armed scavengers roamed openly with swords and shotguns, faces obscured by helmets. Not a single police drone was in sight, but this laxness was deceptive.

Tulsi Hills had private security contractors and there was a geosynchronous satellite in the sky with an operational rail gun painting the borders. There were little digital posters explaining this at various points on the approach road, it being apparently illegal to shoot travelers with a rail gun from the sky without adequate warning. The scavengers were ants, not worthy of that flickering light from space that erased blemishes on the earth, cosmetic surgery on a grand scale.

The road ended in a small copse of trees and a discreet wrought-iron gate. This gate, while symbolic, was still enough to stymie them. An ancient, wobbly butler drone came out. His black carbon-steel body was scratched and dented from various half-hearted attacks by street children whose favorite game was to try to ambush the drone with slings.

Their car stopped in the designated space and the butler scanned their Echos doubtfully.

"It says you're invited to number four," he said, clearly upset by this news. He lit a route on the car's old-school dashscreen. "Please do not deviate from the path, the weapon systems are all live."

The iron gates swung open. It was noticeably cooler inside, and the air gauge switched abruptly from red to green. The tree-lined avenue was broad and largely empty, those other rare vehicles moving above them sleek and black-tinted. There was no noise but the trilling of birds, no people at all, just spotless expanses of grass and trees. The houses themselves were huge and spaced out on either side, all of them barred by individual walls, some still visible through opaque gates.

"Look at the sky!" Gola said. She had rolled down her window. "How the fuck is it a different color?"

Kundo craned his neck. It was bright blue with a few white clouds, something out of a fairy tale. The best Karma usually managed outside was a variation of gray. There was an actual hazy demarcation up there, as if some giant craftsman had spliced together two different watercolors of the sky.

"Breathe the air," Fara said, her mouth wide open.

It was cold and fresh and lightly scented with flowers, so beautiful that the first lungful brought tears to his eyes, and his body unclenched in a way that told him he had never breathed real air before.

"Wow. They get this all the time," Fara said.

Hafez and Gola exchanged glances.

"How many warm bodies do you need to make this much nanotech?" Hafez asked.

"Like maybe a basement full of guys in comas," Gola said.

"Yeah, like three thousand of them, maybe."

They stopped at number four and just stared. The gate was vine-covered, with enough gaps to see a vast expanse of grass within, shaded by two aged mango trees bearing fruit. Birdcalls came from the branches; he saw ravens and sometimes the winking green of parrots. A kingfisher streaked past, indicating some body of water within. In the distance was a many-tiered house, vaguely Moghul in architecture, with open verandas running across the front of each floor.

"Wow. That's a fucking house," Gola said.

"We *give* them all of this," Hafez said, choking with helpless rage. "Don't ever forget that. We break ourselves so they can live like this."

Fara gave him a little hug. "Can you imagine raising kids in this house? Playing in the trees?" She was blinking back tears.

"You think they'd ever let zeros live here?" Hafez said. "Not if we were the last people on earth. Their precious satellites would burn us to ash before we even touched the grass."

Even the chauffer was intimidated. He turned into the lane and honked hesitantly. There was no Echo scan, no drone, nothing smart. The gate swung open seemingly of its own volition. The driveway was lined with pebbles, and cleaved straight to the house, wide enough for two cars side by side. There were no other vehicles up front. Everything looked abandoned.

"Go on in," Kundo said. "We're expected."

The front door was made of priceless real wood, carved with flower motifs. It looked ancient and warped, like the rest of the mansion. Up close the dereliction simply magnified the grandeur, like wandering into an abandoned copse to find it littered with rubies and emeralds. What manner of creature was this, who could afford to strew his wealth about so carelessly?

The six of them waited at the door, uncertain how to proceed without any electronic aid. There was a bronze bell by the frame, aged with verdigris, and when Kundo reached for it he found that the clapper had been removed. Gola tapped her machete against the lock, her legs tensed to push in. Kundo almost felt the Tiger, off to the side, caressing that snub-nosed shotgun, ready and loaded in the overcoat pocket, and realized that his senses were being subtly overlaid by the djinn riding him. ReGi was tense in his brain, a coiled spring, and he could feel her distortion field threaten to cut loose.

There was a gap between the door and the marble floor; the denizens of the mansion did not care to seal their chambers. They didn't give a fuck about keeping the precious good air inside, because there wasn't any good or bad air here; it was all fucking pristine. The sheer unthinkable luxury of that made him stagger. He saw a shadow cross the gap and felt his muscles bunch up.

Then, when the urge to violence was becoming unbearable and Gola was about to kick in the door, it swung open, and a short woman beamed up at them, crinkly eyed, with the comforting waft of onions, a few missing teeth, and an actual broom in her hand.

Kundo looked down and groaned. It was the damn curry lady.

Chapter Eighteen

Chicken Curry at the Death House

Just like that, they were in a sunny kitchen with long stone countertops and a big window that looked out into the back garden, itself a riot of plants and flowers, chaotic compared to the front but far more magical.

Kundo was set to a chopping board, smashing garlic bulbs and then knifing ginger into exactingly thin slices, making two separate piles of the stuff. He was actually hopeless and it was only judicious pulls by ReGi that saved him from detaching his fingers.

Gola had a killer technique on the onions and was rattling them out in style, although it had taken a group effort to dissuade her from using her machete, the clincher coming when Fara pointed out an old bloodstain on the ricasso.

Sophy was exempt from work but permitted to play with a heap of cast-iron pots and pans, and no one minded the din. Hafez and Fara sat at the kitchen table and offered them advice while drinking cold beers. There was a little pot of purple-and-white chrysanthemums on the table. Hafez's gun sat incongruously next to it.

The Curry Lady had a stone mortar and pestle. She showed them how to make a paste out of some of the garlic, ginger, and onions. All the ingredients were laid out in little tin bowls. There was cardamom, cinnamon, and cloves in one, exotic names that conjured up images of spice ships and ancient places long blown to dust. In one large bowl pieces of chicken were marinating in yogurt and salt and sugar, plus some of the ginger-garlic-onion paste. Kundo knew instinctively that this was from a real live animal, rather than a vat-grown substitute.

When the prep work was done they all hovered around the Curry Lady as she began. No one had ever seen cooking like this before, though Kundo had some idea of her unusual style from the cart. There was a vat tucked away in the corner of the kitchen, but it was gathering dust, the manufacturer's seal still intact. This was going to be 100 percent by hand.

The Curry Lady heated oil in the pan, and then dropped in the garlic, ginger, and onions. The room filled with fragrant heat as the aromatics sizzled. She added a cinnamon stick, some cardamom, cloves, and splashes of water without measuring.

She dropped in a couple of green chilies, split down the middle, then the chicken.

The smell of frying meat was both repulsive and oddly compelling. He watched with queasy fascination as the chicken browned with the aromatics and the oil. In a separate pan, the Curry Lady was frying potatoes she had peeled, cubed, and lightly dusted with a flour-and-salt mixture. She dumped them into the curry after a while, and then cooked them together with the chicken. She tasted it with a pinky and then added salt and sugar, and finally stirred in further yogurt. The curry was now simmering over the level of the chicken and potatoes, taking on a beautiful yellowy-brown color. She lowered the top and abruptly cut off the overwhelming miasma of curry.

They took a deep breath, as if some spell were broken.

"So that's lunch, then," Gola said.

"Rice, chicken curry, and salad," the Curry Lady said. "Simple food."

Afterward they sat down to eat in the sunny kitchen, surrounded by pots and pans and herbs flowing from overhead tubs, encased in the aroma of cooking, rice and chicken curry and salad and cold water, and if it was to be their last meal it was certainly their best.

They ate in the old-fashioned way, with their hands, and the Curry Lady showed them how to fold the rice into little bundles with bits of potato and chicken, to much hilarity and then focused effort as their taste buds overruled their squeamishness.

"I came here to fight," Hafez said, nonplussed. "Instead we are eating real food."

The Curry Lady patted his arm. "The master provides," she said.

Kundo raised his eyes. "You found him, then? Your savior?"

"Yes."

"Where is he? Your Horus? Is this his house?"

"Ask him yourself, Kundo Shaheb," the Curry Lady said. "He will come."

"How long have you been here?" Kundo asked. "How many others have come to this house?"

"I am a pilgrim just like you, Kundo Shaheb," she said. "He will answer your questions."

When he came the room shrank. The sun seemed to dim. Here finally was the monster they expected. He was abnormally tall, as he walked on someone else's legs, and his trousers ended somewhere below the knee, revealing long mahogany shins. His open gray coat revealed a torso riven with fiery wounds, the edges burnt black, the seams still showing a dull orange.

But it was his face that arrested Kundo. It was so *human. Ordinary,* even. He looked an old and tired devil, irritable rather than threatening, and his eyes had a glimmer of humor and reluctant curiosity, as if he still found the world endearing after all this time.

Unbidden, Sophy wriggled out of her seat and rushed toward him. She seized a leg and started knocking it with her fist. It made the solid thumping noise of hardened wood.

The devil scooped her up and put her on his shoulder. Naturally, she grabbed his horns for balance, two worn stubs protruding where his hairline started.

"Oh god, so sorry," Fara said, aghast. "Sophy! Get down immediately!"

"No need," Horus said. "I find children delightful."

To eat? Kundo rose off his seat, half in greeting, half to somehow retrieve Sophy.

"Please, don't get up," Horus said. "I will pull up a chair instead."

Which he did, dragging one halfway across the kitchen with one hand while holding his charge tightly in place with the other. Kundo struggled to reconcile this frightening and bizarre creature with the devil's completely unassuming behavior. He noticed that ReGi had gone completely still in his mind, as if hiding.

"Master," the Curry Lady said. She was all aflutter.

"Ah, is that chicken korma I see? Anything left?"

There was shamefully very little left, despite the fact that they had, by Kundo's estimate, murdered at least three live chickens.

"Um, one piece here," Gola said doubtfully, looking at the platter.

"Delightful, pass it over please. It's really the curry and the potatoes I like," Horus said. He was heaping rice onto his plate. "Don't care much for meat." He set Sophy on the floor, where she seemed content to clutch his ragged coat.

He's a bloody vegetarian.

What followed was the strangest ten minutes of their lives, as they sat openmouthed and watched him spoon up rice and chicken curry with gusto. Kundo noticed that he ate the salad but ejected the French beans with a little moue of distaste.

"Excellent, as always, dear," he said, finally wiping his mouth with a napkin.

The Curry Lady beamed.

"So." He looked around the table. "You're the latest lot of winners, eh?"

"Um, yes, what exactly have we won?" Fara said.

"Haven't you heard the stories on the street?" Horus smiled. "The devil has a way out. . . ."

"Where are they?" Kundo asked.

Horus looked up, confused. Kundo, in the process of shoving pictures across the ether, realized that neither of them had a working Echo.

Gola pulled up the pictures on her handheld.

"Ah," Horus said.

"My wife," Kundo said, tapping the screen.

"I remember her," Horus said. "Very spirited lady."

"Did she play the game?"

"Yes," Horus said. "So did the fat man."

"Hassem," Kundo said. He leaned back with a sigh. "So, this is where she ended up. This house." *I've found her.*

"Yes."

"Is she alive?" Kundo asked.

Horus frowned. "I suppose so, why?"

"What do you do with them, you fucker?" Hafez asked. His hands were trembling but he had the gun pointed in the right direction. "What's the scam?"

Horus slumped in his chair. "You think I've got them locked up in a basement somewhere. I'm drinking their blood or turning them into zombies, right?"

"Well?" Hafez asked.

"Really? Do you think that's fun for me?"

"Where are they, then?" Kundo asked. "I want to see them."

"Ah. Well. The invitation is for one." Horus pointed at Fara. "The winner of the game. Believe me, there is a good reason I do not take passengers. The road to the final destination is unpleasant."

"We hacked the game," Fara said. "All of us together."

"I see."

"I mean, we came to find Hassem and Kundo's stupid wife," she said. "We're not Road-heads. We thought it was a scam. But you're a real djinn. So I don't know what to believe now."

"We'll go together or not at all," Hafez said. "And maybe we'll find out if djinns are bulletproof."

"Oh, put that thing away," Horus said. "Really, does it look like I'm dying to take you anywhere? You came here of your own accord. I'm looking for hale and hearty people, champions, not a menagerie of the infirm. However, I think I will make an exception. It just so happens I am in need of a painter."

"I told him about you," the Curry Lady said with a beaming smile.

"A court painter, as it were, someone to chronicle our momentous doings, a veteran hand to capture us in full glory, for posterity and so on, and let me tell you, it's not easy to get me quite right, the angle of the light makes such a big difference, of course, I'm ready to stand for a portrait any time, we would naturally start with me, I understand you carry your instruments with you at all times. . . ."

"He's a djinn, all right," ReGi whispered in Kundo's head.

"You want me to paint you?" Kundo asked. "Like, right now?"

"You'd be our official court artist! Emissary status, too," Horus said. "All of djinndom will acknowledge you. Let me tell you, we don't hand out those like chips."

"He's being serious," ReGi said. "He actually wants . . . a portrait."

"Is he important . . . in djinndom? He sounds like a pompous ass."

"He has many names. Horus the Light. Givaras Maker. Givaras the Broken. The Mad Djinn. Yes, he actually is rather important. He's one of our bêtes noires." ReGi didn't sound scared exactly. Just careful. "To tell you the truth, I did *not* expect him to turn up. No one told me I'd be running up against lunatic elder djinn. He's been missing for years. Everyone's been speculating what the hell he's been up to."

"Everyone?"

"The rest of . . . djinndom. Kundo."

"Hmm?"

"I'd rather he didn't know I was riding you."

"I gathered. You kind of tightened up like a . . . sphincter."

"Thanks. Dick."

"Lord Horus. Sir. Umm, Your Djinnship."

"Horus is sufficient."

"I take the job and you take us all there? Where the others went?"

"Correct."

"I've not painted in three years," Kundo said. "Just to be clear. I'm not sure I can, anymore."

"Don't worry," the djinn said. "The place we are going has a way of . . . livening people up."

Kundo looked around at his crew. "Let's go, then."

Chapter Nineteen

Up the Stairs and Around the Corner

The djinn led them up a grand spiral staircase at the heart of the mansion. It was white marble, chipped and veined with blue, a column of white that went up for seven floors, and as they climbed Kundo saw the encroachment of time stamped on the great halls, the gentle ruin of grandeur, from slipcovered furniture to water damage, the air growing musty from neglect and rotted curtains, great hanging silks bleached pale by the sun, abandoned rattan settees falling apart, then thick layers of dust as even the pretense of usage was gone, and furnishings gave way to increasingly bizarre detritus of past lives.

Still they climbed, and it seemed to Kundo that it was more stairs and floors than the mansion could possibly have held, that in the lee of the great djinn's stride their senses were warped and time itself was slower or faster, that sometimes his feet went uphill and sometimes down. He felt disoriented, wretched, nauseated.

"Do not lose heart," ReGi said. "It is like this in the

wake of powerful djinn, and he is one of our eldest. The distortion field around him makes humes sick."

Kundo gritted his teeth and followed, half expecting the others to call for rest, but Gola had her sygnal slapped to her neck and climbed with her eyes closed, and Hafez had a speed patch on either wrist and the pulse at his temple fluttered like an insect trapped beneath his parchment skin. Kundo and Fara took turns carrying Sophy, and it was only the child who felt nothing of the miasma of the djinn, the field of power that he so casually extruded like a tattered cloak.

"This house was not this tall," Hafez said finally. His color was ashen, and he was leaning openly on Gola, her wide shoulders pulling more than half his weight.

"Ninety-nine floors," Horus said absently. "It was seven stories when I got it, I believe."

"You didn't think to put in an elevator?" Fara asked.

"Do not worry, your aches and pains will fade away once we reach our destination." He spared a glance back.

"Djinns love towers," ReGi said in Kundo's head.

When Horus finally stopped they staggered onto a dirt-choked hall that seemed completely abandoned. There were no machines and no people. It looked more derelict than any place Dead Gola had ever squatted in.

"Where the fuck are the people?" Hafez snarled, his fury barely a whisper.

"That blue door." Horus pointed.

The door shimmered. It was blue and warded with the hand of Fatima. There was graffiti around it, symbols of eyes, overlaid on interlocking geometric patterns that flowed like alien script. They wandered up to it unbidden, drawn by whatever force lived on the other side.

"Be very careful," ReGi whispered urgently. "It's not a door."

"Come, my children." Horus clicked it open. "Welcome to the Black Road."

Kundo hesitated at the edge of the abyss. There was only darkness. He felt the irrational fear that someone would push him from the back. As his eyes adjusted he saw a road below, cleaving through the darkness, itself shaped in black stone, stinking of antiquity, not so much a method of traversal as a conscious wound, imposed on unsuspecting flesh and even now fraying at the edges.

"What fuckery is this?" Hafez shouldered Kundo aside. His face was tight with exhaustion. His gun leapt in his hand like a wide-bore cannon, thrumming with eagerness. "Banchod, this road leads to hell. I'm going to put a hole in you, djinn."

"You thought it was a game," Horus said. "My children, I offer you an *actual* exit. Leave this wretched airless slum. Leave this drowning world. Leave this entire decaying universe. I give you the road to the eternal city. Gangaridai."

"A fairy story for children!" Hafez snarled.

"Let me tell you," Horus said. "Millenia ago, in the age of djinn and man, before the elders withdrew, there was the first city, made by djinn and human hybrids, called the Nephilim. There were other ancient places, but Gangaridai was the best and most glorious, the perfect jewel. When the High King looked into the future, he saw his precious city falling, and misliking the vagaries of time he chose the insane path of removing the city from this realm altogether. What he did, exactly, no one knows, but this place on the other side of the door is more fundamental, more real than our own universe, and there is no time and no decay, and all things exist in their perfect form."

"*Pfft*. Paradise, then. Fairy stories."

Horus smiled. "Paradise? Not exactly. Perhaps it was what he intended, but it did not turn out that way for him. When I found it, the city was dead. Perfectly preserved, but uninhabited."

"The people you take? It's for the city, then? They're all alive?"

"Every single one," Horus said. "Alive and well, living their perfect life in Gangaridai. Each one stepped through this door of their own accord. Every single one wished for a new life, *a new existence,* and I have delivered. Let it not be said that the elder djinn do not keep their promises."

Is he bullshitting?

"He's telling the truth," ReGi said. "That is not a door, it's a hole punched into someplace we are not supposed to go. Kundo, it's not *of this universe.* This thing has to be closed. It's beyond dangerous. These fools have no idea what they're playing at. Do *not* go through."

"This is insane," Fara said. She was staring into the darkness, mesmerized. "We have to go and look, don't we?"

"We've come this far," Hafez said. "Let's go see this city."

They looked at Kundo. He stepped through and fell.

There was dim ambient light. The surface was hard and he could see it was an actual paved road with texture and an edge beyond which the darkness was a lush curtain, thick with the promise of abnegation. The others came through and Horus carefully closed the door. On this side the wood was dark, and it faded from view as soon as Horus let go. Alarmingly. There were no landmarks to mark the spot.

It was alien. The sense of wrongness persisted in every detail, from the sky to the surface to the air pressure. Not inimical. Not threatening. Simply alien. At the same time he realized that Horus had spoken the truth. The aches and exhaustion were fading. He felt stronger, more vital than he ever remembered. There was a sudden itch in his mind, long forgotten, a once natural urge to put pen to paper, or ink to canvas, the urge to create something, *anything*.

Around him, the others were embracing a similar revival. Strength. Vitality. Clarity. The sygnal scarab literally fell off Gola's neck, of its own volition. It was as if the alien air was scouring away all the detritus of ill decisions and bad luck, all the damage life had inflicted on them on a cellular level, returning them to the primal state of grace.

This is what we would have been, if we had not taken countless wrong turns. What magic is this? Has the djinn put us in some machine? Are we in reality covered in worms in some dark room? I swear I remember every step I've taken up to the door. What the hell is this?

Horus looked at them knowingly, let them enjoy the moment.

"What is this?" Hafez asked finally. "We're not in Chittagong anymore."

"This is the actual Black Road. What you see in the game is a facsimile," Horus said. "Yes, we are not in Chittagong, not on earth, not even in our dear old universe. Look at the horizon."

"The city," said Kundo. "Just like the game."

"Gangaridai. *My* city. The first city of man and djinn. Removed here by ways and means beyond our current comprehension. I am trying to . . . liven it up."

"To bring it to life, you mean? How?"

"With people, of course," said Horus. "Your people. I did not kill them or drink their blood or whatever nonsense people say about me. I gave them a path to a new world. I let them choose. Every single person here *chose* to stay."

Kundo looked at his fellows. They looked invigorated, as if already, their stamp on this reality was greater than the drowning world they had left behind.

"Walk with me, Kundo," Horus said. "The love you seek is in the city. What do you have to lose?"

There was only one direction to go. Kundo led them, with Sophy on his shoulders. Fara followed, then Gola helping Hafez, with the djinn in the rear, for protection, apparently. From what, exactly?

"What the hell are those lumps?" Kundo asked. The light wasn't exactly great, the source ethereal, although a good deal seemed to be coming off the city walls ahead.

"Bodies," Hafez said flatly.

Easily verified a minute later, when they crossed the first mound. They had been evidently dragged and piled up together, perfectly preserved. It was impossible to say how old they were, but signs of violence marred them: smashed-in faces, torsos carved in half, splintered rib cages. Ludicrously, it reminded him of the game.

"So many dead." Fara hugged her daughter tight and tried to shield her sight. "All the way to the gates."

"The original citizens," Horus said. "It is not certain what killed them. Fear not, my friends, these atrocities were committed many millennia ago."

"They're fresh corpses," Fara said. "And it looks like someone's been moving them around."

"Yes, we've been trying to sort them. Sort of a civic service from the new inhabitants of the city, although you can see we are dreadfully shorthanded," Horus said. "Any errant beasts who wander here must also be dealt with, of course."

"I'm sorry, errant what? Are we likely to be attacked?" Kundo asked.

"Denizens of other universes have stumbled into this space from time to time. Violence is possible but fear not, the city has defenses."

"It didn't seem to have helped the original people much," Hafez said. "This is a bloody massacre."

"Yes, well, I wasn't in charge back then. I grant you that the road to Gangaridai is somewhat unpleasant," Horus said. "But you'll love it once you get there. And aren't you all feeling much, *much* better? More puissant, hmm?"

They had to agree that they did, in fact, feel far livelier than they ever had. The bodies were disconcerting but there were no flies or rot or decay, robbing them of much of the visceral impact of corpses, this realm not accepting any of the accoutrements of death that normally offended the senses.

"Plenty of bodies here for Hassem to raise," Gola said after a while. Fara made a gagging noise.

"Ah, yes, Hassem." Horus grinned. "A true deviant. We have given him more suitable toys to play with. I assure you, he is calm here, and useful. Fear not, children, this place is more timeless than paradise and a mite more interesting."

Chapter Twenty

Something Interesting

Horus proved prophetic, because something interesting hit them as soon as they reached the bend in the road within five hundred yards of the city; close enough to see the gates open, too far away to make a run for it. A yellow-tinged mist obscured the edges of their path, accompanied by three short bursts of a trumpet. Suddenly armored figures clambered over the sides, somehow flipping into view as if they had been walking the mirror surface below. They seemed vaguely humanoid, and when they snapped into attention with their pila and their long shields, it was clear that they were, in fact, Roman legionnaires.

"From the lost legion of Marcus Crassus," Horus said. "A bloody pain. God knows how they've ended up here, but they've been pestering us for years. Won't listen to reason, either."

The cohort lined up frighteningly fast and advanced like a threshing machine, six lines of spearheads thrust up

in a staggered, serrated edge, shields held ready to inter-
lock. It was not a full testudo but close enough.

Horus shrugged his way forward. The cohort snarled
with rage, seeming to recognize him. Latin insults were
hurled at the djinn from the front line of grinning soldiers. The Primus Pilus raised his short sword and
pointed at the djinn, mouthing a command. His great
helm was adorned with the tawny fur of a lion, somewhat
tattered with age but still quite stylish.

The five hundred trained men of the first cohort
ground to a halt, the large shields of the front line slam-
ming onto the floor with an impressive boom. Soldiers in
the fifth and sixth ranks readied their pila to throw. Others behind them had slings.

They were close enough to see smoky black lines
drawn on the weapons and armor of the legionnaires, interlocking geometric shapes similar to the door, in fact. It
gave the soldiers an unearthly air at odds with their obvious brutal efficiency.

The Signifier came forward, the standard bearer of the
cohort and traditionally their luckiest member, in charge
of making bargains with the gods and any other cosmic
powers the legion might encounter. The cohort's standard was a shaman's head mounted on a stick, the face
bleached and withered but still very much alive.

The eyes of the shaman head flipped open and he

screamed an incoherent stream of rage and pain. The yellow smog came out of his nose and mouth, thickening around the Signifier, and then across to encompass the entire front lines of the cohort, coating the soldiers entirely. The Primus gave another shout and the front lines started a very slow lurch forward.

"Shit," Horus said. "It's the first cohort. They've gone feral."

Hafez leveled his gun and fired. The boom made everyone flinch. Thirty yards away the Signifier staggered and then righted himself. They could see his bestial grin. The head atop his spear continued screaming.

"What the fuck?" Hafez snarled.

"He's protected," Horus said absently. "The head is creating a distortion field. They've got some tricks, these Romans. Very adaptable people. Of course, Marcus Crassus knew djinns very well; he must have imparted our secrets to his legates."

Horus was gathering his own distortion field, the particle-altering effect all djinns carried about them, their patrimony from god or whatever quirk of evolution had birthed their race. He created a windmilling motion, his high frame tottering as a breeze intensified behind him. The djinn wind smashed into the yellow haze, diverting some of it up. It did not noticeably slow the advance of the soldiers.

"Look!" ReGi jerked Kundo's head up. He felt his eyes tighten as the djinn did something to his vision, and he could see through the haze, past the cohort, up the slope of the road, where the city gates had swung wide open. Hunting horns sounded a jaunty tune over the thrumming of hooves. The entire road shook from the impact of steel-shod destriers, and the cohort paused in its tracks, barely a dozen yards from the djinn. A host of cavalry advanced from the city, their bronze armor catching glints of ambient light. They carried lanterns on their horses and it looked from afar like a charge of fireflies.

Kundo could see the tips of their lances streaming multicolored pennants as they lowered in a deliberate wave. The Romans did not seem particularly worried. A laconic command from the Primus Pilus prompted his men into action. The back half of the cohort swung around with practiced ease and presented a testudo to the approaching cavalry. The Signifier glared at Horus and turned his magic decapitated head around, focusing his power at the new enemy. The legionnaires facing them remained in place, unconcerned. One of them blew Gola a kiss and mimed something vulgar.

Kundo watched, aghast, as the two groups collided with percussive force, cavalrymen and Romans tossed into the air from the initial impact. The first Roman line crumpled, but the second and third lines stiffened up and held, turning the battle into a pushing match. Without much room to maneuver the cavalry was now left flailing ineffectually at the soldiers from atop their horses, while Roman pila stabbed at their armored mounts with tinny blows. The yellow haze did not seem to disturb the cavalry much, although Kundo could see it corroding their pennants and tabards.

The legionnaires began pulling down the horsemen, organizing into teams of three or four to muscle the riders down. The rear half of the knightly force, without much to do, began to edge back to attempt another charge. It was a mess of a battle, neither force wanting to fall off the edge, neither able to really come to grips with the enemy in the narrow space.

The Primus Pilus did not like his losses, however, for in the temporary lull in the melee the Cornicen (hornblower) sounded the note for retreat. The haze thickened as before and the first cohort shrank together and then split in two, scuttling like insects over the edge of the road to the mirror surface below. Within minutes they were gone, taking their fallen with them, leaving behind only the corpses of the armored horsemen and their broken lances.

It was a surprisingly quick battle. The remaining cavalrymen swung around wordlessly and galloped back through the gates. The road to the city was uncontested once more.

Hafez rapped his knuckles on the nearest fallen knight. He lifted the helm, peered at the face.

"Machines," he said finally. "They're made of clock-work."

Kundo walked over. The road was slick with oil, not blood. Sapphire cogs and bent gears lay whirring in the armored head, giving off smoke. The brass was not armor but the skin itself of the cavalryman, polished to a mirror finish, now bent and pocked with blows from the Roman pila.

"Clockwork horses and clockwork men," Kundo said.

"The city has defenses," Horus said. "What we need are operators."

"Gamers . . . ," Fara said.

"Precisely." Horus beamed at them. "I told you it was fun here."

Chapter Twenty-One

Towering Above

Horus took them to the tallest tower, naturally. It would be against his nature to reside anywhere else. The city itself was a stunning amalgamation of towers and copper domes, of unlikely fountains and profligate flouting of natural laws such as gravity and thermodynamics. Sequestered in a sunless realm, light itself rose profusely from random sources, riots of color in defiance of the oppressive blackness of the road.

To Kundo's disbelieving eyes it was impossible to separate magic from technology. Numbed by the ongoing presence of djinn and other fantastical things, they were all beginning to accept the wonders before them at face value, with almost phlegmatic ease.

Looking down, he could see certain areas crowded with people, lit from lamps and in places walls that glowed, but many more quarters of the vast city were dark and deserted entirely.

People, Kundo thought with a nervous thrill. People

taken from Chittagong. Not taken, precisely. These were pilgrims who had followed the djinn's beacon, those who saw him as a messiah, people come to claim the promise of a new world, as people always did, no matter what they left behind. It was the nature of humans, wasn't it, to yearn for the new?

"There is a telescope in the east balcony," Horus said to him. "If you were to look down past the dolphin fountain, you would see a smithy, an artificer's workshop, you might call it. Observe it for a time and you might see whom you've come here for."

Kundo walked with leaden feet to the instrument, his heart beating uncomfortably fast. He felt the familiar churning anxiety in his stomach, except now, at the fruition of his labor, it was magnified tenfold. Fara touched his arm as he went past her, but he barely felt it.

The east balcony looked down at a square centered around a stone dolphin that floated above a jet of water, shifting poses. Kundo ignored this miracle of engineering and spotted the shop front. There was a glow from the window, from a forge. A man lounged on a bench outside, a tankard in his hand. Kundo watched him for several long minutes. The man shouted at someone through the window after a while, and then laughed at the response. He was handsome enough and seemed entirely too comfortable. Did this lout have nothing better to do?

Then she came out. Her hair was tied back, sweaty. She was wearing a heavy leather apron, and her arms were bare. They were corded with muscle. Had they always been like that? He couldn't remember her ever picking up anything heavier than a book. She carried a hammer in her left hand and a short sword in her right. *A sword? She was the blacksmith?* She oiled the sword with practiced sweeps of a rag and wrapped it in a piece of burlap, tying the bundle with string. She handed the package to the waiting man.

He doffed an imaginary hat at her and left. He did not look back. She didn't spare him a second glance, either.

He's just a customer. Kundo felt immense relief. Alone now, she sat down on the vacant bench, resting. He could see her chest move up and down as she drew long breaths. She tapped her hammer idly against her booted foot. There was an easy competence about her, as if these lost years had bequeathed her a host of skills. Kundo remembered her hesitant, ill at ease with her own grace. This was some other creature, wholly unconcerned, reveling in physical labor, emanating an aura of animal vitality.

"Is this real?" he asked ReGi, half-afraid of the answer.

"Yes," the djinn said. "It's all real, Kundo."

He watched her through the night. Or was it day? She worked and rested alternately, and received customers bringing her broken things. Her work was mundane and simple, he saw. Bent swords, spearheads, parts for the copper knights injured in the battle, or other simple tools. Once she produced a modern-looking wrench, once something more delicate, like a child's toy. She came outside frequently; the smithy must have been stifling.

Throughout his vigil Kundo prayed, *Let there be no one, let there be no one.* No lover to claim a kiss. No "friend" to slip into the backroom. No one to hang by the window, gossiping while she worked, easy camaraderie that would one day become love. There was no one. She seemed solitary and completely content, responding to passersby with grunts, most often ignoring the world around her. There was no one.

It was many hours later when a cramp attacked his leg that he realized how long he had watched her. He got up. There was something like relief in his core, a heavy knot being loosened. He walked back to find the others still waiting for him.

"Well, man? Have you found her finally?" Hafez asked.

"She's there," Kundo said to Fara. "She's working as a blacksmith. She's strong."

"I'm glad you found her," Fara said with a smile.

"She looks well, doesn't she?" Horus asked.

"Yes, she does."

"This place, there is no entropy, you understand? No time. You can live forever here, perfect, *pristine*," Horus said. "Why should you face the indignities of the world left behind, that wrecked, drowning place run by distant gods? You can slough off that skin and become new.

"We have tunneled here into a more fundamental part of reality. The universe we lived in is a mere skin, a surface dream. We are in the meat and bones of it now; your life force is more potent here, your gifts are greater. You can paint in this life, Kundo, better than you've ever painted. You can capture the wonder and the magnificence of this place. You *will be famous. You will win her heart again!*

"Your friends . . . Fara the champion. Our barracks are full of clockwork knights. There are not enough of us capable of operating them. We *need* you. Defend the city that is your birthright, unleash your true spirit. Be *useful* once again.

"Dead Gola, you would not suffer so here. This realm is deathless. That tick in your brain that called for sygnal is gone now, surely you can feel it? You were never meant to be that way. The city is full of machines and mysteries, gears that only a mind like yours can penetrate. Be the genius you were meant to be, before addiction ruined you.

"Tiger Hafez, do you not feel the strength returning to your limbs? Can you feel the cloud lifting from your brain? Your disease is arrested here. You have seen the enemies we face. You will fight again. You will face the Signifier of the first cohort once more, and the next time, your gun will shoot true, for I will etch my sigil on your bullets."

"Your words are sweet, Horus," Kundo said. "We were broken before, and now we will be remade perfect. It is convenient we found you."

"They call me Horus the Broken," the djinn said. "Look at my body, Kundo. Do I look whole to you? I know pain better than anyone. Do you think I would sell you false promises? To live is to break. But not here. You get a second chance, man, an impossible gift in a *new universe.*"

"Well?" Kundo looked at his friends. "What do you guys say?"

"I'd get more time." Hafez shrugged like it meant nothing to him. "One more fight."

"I could stay," Gola said. She was touching her neck absently. "No junkies in paradise, huh?"

Kundo's eyes went to Fara, who simply nodded. Then his eyes strayed to Sophy, fast asleep in her mother's arms, perfectly unconcerned that they had crossed out of all known time and space.

"No time here, Horus," he whispered. "What happens to her, then?"

"She stays the same, the perfect child," Horus purred.

"We can't do that to her," Kundo said. "Don't you understand? She'd never get to grow up."

"You'd save her all the pain and sorrow."

"She wouldn't get to live."

"She looks perfectly happy now."

"That's a hideous choice," Kundo said. "We can't do that to her."

"It's all right Kundo. I'll take her back," Fara said. "Don't worry. You guys stay. I wasn't going to stay here anyway. Nothing really for me."

"No . . ."

"You came all this way for your wife, Kundo," Fara interrupted him. "You crossed the fucking universe. Stop being a pussy and go out there and get her. Tell her all the shit you've ever wanted to say. I can't believe you're even sitting here talking about it. Go, dude."

"Yeah, I found her. I watched her," Kundo said. He struggled to find the right words, but he felt lighter than he had in months. "You're right, there were a lot of things I wanted to say. But the thing is, I'm not sure she needs to hear them. She looks happy here. Complete. Better than she's ever been back home, that I can remember. She didn't run away with anyone. She just . . . chose another road."

Chapter Twenty-two

Memorial

They were on a tower again, on the rooftop this time. Thirty floors below them, black water lapped the edges of the building with shallow waves. The entire ground floor was deluged now, a state of permanence rather than encroachment. There were no more streets here, only canals, plied by boatmen in goggles and long oars.

Kundo sat in a deck chair, a cold beer in his hand. There was a cooler by his feet with ice and at least a few more bottles. Dead Gola sat next to him, drinking in companionable silence, as was her wont. She had a joint in her left hand, in lieu of the sygnal. ReGi regularly sent her bags and bags of organic weed. She took a few tokes and offered it to Kundo, who waved her off. By her feet lay her machete and Hafez's gun.

It was for Hafez that they were on the roof today. It was the first anniversary of his death. He had refused to return to the hospital. One afternoon he had set his accounts in order and shot himself.

Fara and ReGi fussed over the little shrine they had erected. There were real flowers and a bottle of whiskey. Ron the bartender had supplied the booze and snacks. He sat next to Kundo and stared yearningly at Fara.

Sophy had shot up in the past eighteen months and now spoke incessantly. She had drawn a picture for Uncle Hafez and insisted on explaining it to everyone. They had grieved at his funeral, but one year on it was a more festive affair. People on neighboring rooftops waved and promised to visit. Steel-silk rope bridges connected all of them, the few that remained. They had given up the streets to the water, and lived in the sky now.

Fara called them over when she was finally ready. They took sips of the whiskey. She recited a short poem for the Tiger, from his namesake the Persian poet. Gola fired off a round in the air, a heavy incendiary shot trailing djinn hellfire, the bullet etched with the sigils of Horus. Hafez had chosen his own way out, but his gun remained and so a piece of him lived on. The bullet streaked into the air and then exploded, showering the sky with fire.

The people next door cheered. There was no alarm. Karma had withdrawn. Horus had taken too many people away, taken them in droves. As the water rose, the others had left on their own. In the end, there just weren't enough people left to warrant Karma's efforts. She had left without fanfare, a bald message going out for a week letting people know that the administration was coming to an end. There was no one worthwhile left to administer, after all, only zero scum. In the end the revolution had been that simple.

Hafez had lived long enough to see that, at least. It was the last time he had laughed.

The scavengers remained, inheriting a treasure trove, finally claiming the entire run of the place. They plucked their fruit from orchards on the hills. They grew their own plants on rooftop gardens. They scavenged air and water and food from a million dispensers gathering dust, making a new skin on the city, a new tribe, pitifully few but living.

There was one house still occupied in Tulsi, with a blue door that sometimes opened. They were always welcome there and every few months Kundo made the trek over for some chicken curry.

Kundo sat on his rooftop most days and watched the city alone. He painted the hues of the water as it lapped on the stilts of his world. He captured the boatmen who wandered the canals. He imagined the people on other rooftops and gave them names and stories. On festive days, when other people turned up, he got the feeling that it was not quite over yet.

"You regret it?" ReGi asked him, clinking bottles.

"Sometimes," Kundo said. "But not today."

Acknowledgments

For all the people we have lost; I hope there are other worlds where they thrive.

About the Author

SAAD Z. HOSSAIN is a Bangladeshi author writing in English. He lives in Dhaka. His war satire, *Escape from Baghdad!,* was published in 2015, and included in the *Financial Times* best books of 2015. It was translated into French as *Bagdad la Grande Evasion.* This book was a finalist for the Grand Prix de L'imaginaire 2018. His second book, *Djinn City,* was released in 2017, also translated into French. His third, *The Gurkha and the Lord of Tuesday,* was published in 2019 by Tordotcom. It was a finalist for the Locus Award as well as the 2020 IGNYTE Award.

TOR·COM

Science fiction. Fantasy. The universe.

And related subjects.

*

More than just a publisher's website, *Tor.com* is a venue for **original fiction, comics,** and **discussion** of the entire field of SF and fantasy, in all media and from all sources. Visit our site today—and join the conversation yourself.